INVISIBLE ISLANDS

Angus Peter Campbell is a well-established novelist and poet. His novel *An Oidhche Mus do Sheòl Sinn* is considered a modern classic in Scottish literature. A graduate of the University of Edinburgh, he has worked as a kitchen-porter, forester, lobster-fisherman, builders' labourer, journalist and film actor. He is now a full time writer. He was born on the Island of South Uist, spent his teenage years on the Isle of Seil, and now lives on the Isle of Skye. He is married with six children, and has been awarded many literary prizes, including both the Bardic Crown and a Creative Scotland Award in 2001.

Dhan fheadhainn a rinn an do-fhaicsinneach faicsinneach
To all those who shone, like Haggarty, in the dark

INVISIBLE ISLANDS

Angus Peter Campbell

OTAGO

Otago
Copyright Angus Peter Campbell 2006

First published by Otago in 2006

Otago Publishing
355 Byres Road
Glasgow G12 9XZ

A catalogue record for this book is available from the British Library

Typeset by Hope Services (Abingdon) Ltd

ISBN-10 0 9552283 0 1
ISBN-13 978 0 9552283 0 8

www.invisibleislands.com
www.otagosecure.com

'Myth is the hidden part of every story'
Italo Calvino

Many people and memories, especially from my childhood, inhabit these pages. Like a dream remembered, some of it later came into focus, though some was also imagined, or at least hoped for. To all those who were – or became – revelations to me, my belated thanks.

I am particularly indebted to Alexander Carmichael's great work, Carmina Gadelica, which serves as the village well for these writings. My thanks also to Christine Cain, Librarian at Sabhal Mòr Ostaig, for providing reference sources, including the Latin quote from the writer Flavius. I quote from Derick Thomson's very fine poem 'The Scarecrow' on Page 53, and the quote from Christina MacInnes, Eriskay, on the last two pages is taken extant from Fr Allan MacDonald's marvellous collection 'Gaelic Words and Expressions from South Uist and Eriskay'.

My thanks to Morag Ann MacLeod and Highland Council, and Dr Gavin Wallace and the Scottish Arts Council, for the funding of the Iain Crichton Smith Writing Fellowship which I've held for the past three years during which I've written this and other works.

My particular thanks to Andrew Young for his editiorial advice and encouragement. To Lyndsay and the children for their love of life. To Alf Tupper and Limpalong Leslie for the notion that all things were possible. And to John Storey for his great friendship and support. Without them – and many others who remain unmentioned – this book would not exist.

INVISIBLE ISLANDS

1

Liursaigh

In the long archipelago of islands, the people rarely communicated except by satellite on long wintry nights when the distant falling of a star and the constant whine of the rising wind reminded them of their own mortality or immortality.

Then the dead, stirred by the sounds of their own repeated voices on the airwaves, would be reminded by the living that it was All Souls Night or New Year's Eve or Halloween or some other long forgotten festival, and moving instantly through time and space, would find themselves hovering by a lighted window on Sharinsay, or standing by the empty roadside in Eagradail, or running through the walls of what used to be nothing in the now-uninhabited island of St Ronan.

Those left living registered the noises, taking them to be the fresh stirrings of the ascending north wind, or the flap of an old curtain or the faulty automatic clicking of the remote control.

Through the broken windows and beneath the badly fitted doors they crept, the living and the dead, departing with certainties and anxieties, arriving with marvels and doubts. The plea was for dignity and acknowledgement, that it had all been worthwhile.

And so, standing in the doorways, or leaning through the windows, or sitting by the firesides, or travelling along the roads, they began telling each other stories, beginning with the creation of the compass that – they believed – was originally imagined on an antipodean meridian, which made all things eternal and invisible.

The southernmost island in the archipelago – Liursaigh – had been dead and evacuated, but had been re-populated, thanks to the vision and investment of the Department of Re-Population of the Social Wing of Enterprise Europe.

Originally cleared of its indigenous people by MacRuairidh in the middle of the nineteenth century, two shepherd families clung on as tenants beyond the mud war of 14-18, but the fierce winter of 1919 broke their spirits, and some old ghosts (if by chance you happen to meet them at the time of the turning of the tides) will tell you of how they drowned crossing the firth, only yards from what seemed to be safety.

Seconds from safety, these ghosts now drift eternally between the two tides, as if uncertain whether the rising or the falling tide is the better option. Through eternal experience, their hopes are highest – and the subsequent grief the greater – at the Spring and Autumn equinoxes, when the ocean depths push in expectation, then decline in shame. Occasionally, of course, the oceans and the ghosts themselves believe that the impossible will happen, when external events conspire to suggest that this time – this time, surely – the earth will give way and the mountains themselves will fall into the heart of the sea. But each time the waters recede, the equinox passes and the lost tenant farmers resume their infinite journeying between the high and low tides.

The ghosts' best hope lay with global warming, but even that failed to deliver, despite the earthquakes and the droughts and the famines and the shifting ice-floes. Though the Arctic melted and the Antarctic eventually became a lush meadow, those yards from safety were never breached and the island that they left – like the island that they never reached – was possessed by others, briefly alive as they themselves once were.

And so there they were, that night, unaware that Halloween had once again come round, like an old dream.

Ivor, the youngest person on the island, was reading a handed-down comic. In the half-light, Alf Tupper and all his imagined friends were in shadow on the page, chasing the words that ran out of their mouths literally in bubbles to hang suspended in all time.

The words were in English, like pale clouds on the horizon. His mind was a rainbow, but the seven colours failed to illuminate the words, made redundant by the pictures that spelt shock and fear and awe and surprise and delight and joy.

Ivor licked his finger and followed the boxes inside of which were the pictures beside which floated the bubbles with the irrelevant words. One said 'Aaargh!'. One said 'Ouch!'. Another said 'Zooks!'

Outside, the wind roared. Aargh! thought Ivor, without thinking. Ouch! Zooks! And it was a nor-westerly, for he recognized the voice of that wind, the way in which its vocables crowded together, so that it became almost all-vowel: ooooooo and aaaaaaaa and iiiiiiiiii though not entirely vowelized like the north wind, which at its best or worst whined with an incessant uuuuuuuuuuuuuuuuuuuu until the whole world was possessed by it and became that word, that noise, that sound, a singular u.

In the comic, the characters were wearing masks and frightening each other. An old woman was flying on a broom. Lanterns hung in the dark. A small child held his or her older sister's hand. They were walking around in a crowd, each child carrying something: a sack, a walking stick, a hat, a face, a light, an apple, a sickle. In the end box, they were all gathered round a tub in front of a fire, smiling.

If there were other children here, Ivor thought, that's what I would do: walk abroad in a shower of all my days. Walk with them to Rubha Fhionnlaigh where Haggarty, whose clothes were made of gold, lived all by himself, weaving an ever-expanding house out of gathered crotal and kelp.

No one had ever seen Haggarty, of course, because his gold clothing made him invisible by day and blinded the curious by night. But they'd all heard him in the twilight scratching the rocks until they bled red, and moving between the tangle and the seaweed in the light of day when the sound of the wind and the waves drowned his cries and yelps and songs.

'From Ireland' some said of his origins, though others argued Russia, or Egypt or Norway but the less mundane suggested the supernatural, as if heaven or fairy-land could explain the marvel of his existence.

Ivor himself believed that Haggarty had woven himself out of the kelp and crotal first before extending that universe to everything that he touched. Maybe his index finger and his main toe had webbed between lichen growing on a rock and the seaweed emerging from the centre of the earth, and in trying to extricate himself the two had intertwined, and out of that marriage of inconvenience had emerged the knitted person and the woven world he inhabited.

The gold, surely, was the sunlight catching on the kelp in the morning light or the setting sun glistening on the red crotal of his hair as he leapt between sea and rock, between ocean and earth.

The comic, naturally, was called Treasure Island and all who had ever lived on Liursaigh were, of course, convinced that Haggarty was the keeper of the buried treasure. Eight Spanish galleons laden with golden doubloons had once been shipwrecked on the jagged reefs to the north of the island, and there was little doubt that the Atlantic Drift had washed these doubloons – one hundred thousand of them, at the very least, according to De Groot the famous Dutch scholar who had researched the incident – ashore at the very place where Haggarty gathered his crotal and his kelp.

That was no sunlight, therefore, catching on the kelp in the morning light but actual doubloons of Spanish gold woven on to the sealskin that covered Haggarty as he moved in between the light, in the shadows of men's hopes.

And that wasn't the only gold: as MacRuairidh made his great escape west with his prize ship loaded with the clan's possessions, it too came to grief on the very same reefs. It never belonged to him in the first place, the old people said, and if God in His great providence had given it to Haggarty, so be it. MacRuairidh's tapestries, woven in Florence, were said to carpet Haggarty's home and his silver casks and goblets were used as feeding-bowls for the kittiwakes and fulmars which daily descended on Haggarty's abode for their food and drink.

Three ghosts stood outside Ivor's door at that moment, summoned from the north and the east and the west by the airwaves which, that evening, were transmitting an archive programme in Gaelic about the olden days. To celebrate Halloween, the BBC had commissioned a tri-media programme recalling the voices of the long-dead telling how it used to be: Archie telling of how he used to block up the windows of the old people's thatched houses with turf, so that they couldn't recognize morning coming; Flora telling of how she used to spend the entire previous day and evening baking so that there would be enough food for all those who came calling; and Dòmhnall reciting the Fingalian chant – *Duan na Fèinne* – which he used to intone outside each door to gain entrance.

Across time and eternity they heard their own voices recalling the truth and were unable not to move to listen, and here they were standing on the threshold listening to how it had always been, in the telling.

The door, of course, did not stop them, but memory did. None of them could enter until asked, and none of them would be asked until the old ritual was re-enacted. So they listened to themselves, and as they listened began to tell so that Ivor heard not just the voices coming from the internal media around him, but from the outside, outside his very door, rising and falling in sweet cadences despite, or maybe because of, the strong wind.

Thigeabh a-steach – 'Come in', he heard himself say and they swept in, oblivious to one another, each reciting his and her different tale, echoing the tri-media sounds all round the room.

Bhitheadh. Bhithinn a-sin a' fuine fad an latha 's fad na h-oidhche – 'Yes. The entire day would be spent baking' Flora said, from the TV and from the laptop and from the radio and in person, as she stood by the kitchen table.

'S bha meadhan-là ann mus do dh' èirich cuid aca – 'And it was mid-day before some of them woke' laughed Archie, from over by the window-space as the exact words reverberated from the various speakers while Dòmhnall stood silent by the door, his chant having been chanted, and his entrance having been gained.

They'll know, thought Ivor. Without any doubt, they'll know. They'll know whether Alf Tupper, that tough of the track, could really run forever while eating fish and chips. They'll know whether Haggarty has treasure, and silver and gold and a suit made out of doubloons and a carpet made of tapestry and feeding-bowls out of silver-caskets.

He committed the mistake of asking the question, of questioning the myth, of asking the dead something that belonged to the living.

And with that they vanished, without even a puff of mist to signify their existence.

2

Craolaigh

The most loquacious island in the entire archipelago is the Island of Craolaigh, on which no one has ever lived, and on which no one could ever live.

It is basically a lump of molten rock which rises from a ten mile deep base in the Atlantic seabed to a height of 500 feet above water, to a circumference of two miles. Aerial geological photographs have measured the island at 689 metres by 301 metres, including the varying inlets which serrate the eastern edge. It consists largely of shale and Lewissian gneiss, blessed with a half-open oval bowl on top, which may or may not have once been volcanic, according to whichever geologist you happen to listen to.

In any case, no written or oral evidence of any volcanic activity survives, even from the archive material – songs and poems and stories – recorded over the years from the neighbouring island of Clàraigh now lying in digital form with the School of Scottish Studies in Edinburgh.

Not a single song or *duan* (poem) or story from that remarkable archive makes any reference to Craolaigh, which in itself has caused tremendous speculation amongst archivists and folklorists. Was it simply that the tiny rocky outpost of Craolaigh was always considered irrelevant, because uninhabitable? Or are there darker, mythic reasons? Some scholars, for example, suggest that Craolaigh was the actual prototype for *an ifrinn fhuar* (the cold hell) which one had to by-pass on the northern route to *Tir nan Òg* (The Land of the Ever-Young), which lay far to the west.

The concept of a cold rather than a burning hot hell was, of course, pre-Christian, and because so very little has survived from these times, the largely sociological question of what role or function the rocky outpost of Craolaigh ever played in Gaelic life, including its mythology, remains open-ended.

What is certain, however, both from on-land archeo-logical and geological surveys and from extensive aerial photography and analysis, is that no human ever stayed or lived on Craolaigh. It has been the sole reserve of fulmars and kittiwakes and sea-eagles and gannets and all the other winged creatures on God's earth since time began, or at least since the actual volcanic upheaval which tore the rock up from the Canadian Shield and left it visible on the horizon, like a promise or a threat of more to come.

The telecommunications mast which now dominates the island from the air, but which is invisible from land and sea, sheltered as it is within the half-open volcanic bowl, was erected ten years ago by the BBC and Quadbandfon who uniquely combined to erect a bi-system, in direct competition with Murdoch and his allies, who had largely taken the satellite transmission route.

To put it simply, the mast on Craolaigh is the central hub of a vast international telecommunications network: the place where the babble of languages transmitting their loves and joys and pains and griefs and terrors (as well as their detritus of information and advertising – mostly sex products) coalesce and gather, then divide and separate, each to individual ears, homes, computers, laptops, mobiles, hearts and beds.

No indigenous ghosts hang around Craolaigh, so their voices aren't heard in the international exchange which ranges from terrorism to soccer, from penile extensions to the common news of birth, marriages and deaths.

On quiet nights, of course, the insomniacs on the neighbouring islands, ranging from the senile GP to the sleepless young child, hear the hum of the voices moving from and towards all points of the compass, and some imagine that they can detect language in the hubbub, much as in the old days men and women imagined they could see God in the sky or in the earth or in the blossoming flower.

The waking walking passengers on passing ships sometimes imagine too that they hear voices speaking to them in their own language: Arabic to the Arab, Italian to the Italian, Icelandic to the Icelander, though when questioned none of them could recall the actual words, beyond asserting that they were convinced that, yes, the very night the bombs went off in Cairo – or was it Rome or Reykjavik? – they'd heard voices conspiring in the dark, and of course it could have been nothing else but the bombers giving their final signals to one another before the big bang. Hadn't they heard the voices? Hadn't they, in actual fact, even heard the bombs go off in the far distance, like an echo of horror, a premonition of what they now knew to be true?

So the lovers would speak, caressing their mobile phones in Monte Cassino – or was it San Francisco? – slipping out those sensuous words, which turned her wet or him hard, and the kisses, which never quite reached the ear, and the promises and the thrusts and the lies and the excuses, which either condensed distance or extended it beyond repair.

But mostly what passed through Craolaigh was rubbish: the e-mails which are immediately deleted, the property investments which no one wants, the prize won which doesn't exist, as well as the millions of texts and spoken messages telling that he is on the train, or on the bus, or in the car and will be home in ten minutes.

If analyzed, of course, the marvellous archive from the island of Clàraigh would reveal much the same fact: if the archive hadn't been edited and chosen, the same human silt would have gathered, concerning itself with boils and hemorrhoids and lusts and desires and small hopes and failures – with the things which consume the vast majority of our daily lives. If there are great songs and poems and stories and tales and myths and legends and beliefs in the annals, they are there because fortune happened to gather them, in the shape of a passing collector, or a travelling scholar sponsored by a university or a government momentarily distracted from a war or from economic development.

So who gathers these tales that, like the earlier tales, rise out of the silt, emerge out of the chaos, shine out of the darkness? Who distinguishes any more between the babble of voices and the bubble of voices, between this word and that, between this language and the other, between hope and terror, between love and lust, between the truth and the lie, between the sweet promise uttered down the phone from St Tropez, let's say, which is simultaneously heard as a flagrant lie in Madagascar?

No storyteller ever lived on Craolaigh. In a sense, it had no story to tell: its story was always told by someone else, from somewhere else. It was always the story of a visitor, of a stranger, of a passer-by, of a traveller on a passing ship: do you know that Craolaigh is volcanic, sedimentary, gneissian, remote, dangerous, dark, brooding, foreboding, hellish?

The stories they told were the stories that they brought with them, the ones they imagined. In that, they were like the story-tellers and song-makers and reciters of nearby Clàraigh, who also invented an island whose earth was made of magic, whose sky was made of silk, whose people were the best dancers (as well as the best singers and boat-makers) in the whole wide world.

These boat-makers and lovers cry out in the babble, their voices striving to be heard in the cacophony. A young girl sings somewhere – perhaps in Buenos Aires? – and here in Craolaigh her garbled voice is disentangled before being globally distributed, for a subscription fee, to the entire known universe. The same with bodies, histories, fictions, university degrees and weapons: everything from a bare clitoris to a covered Kalashnikov can be revealed, accessed, purchased, used.

On the hard rock of Craolaigh, on which no one has ever lived and on which no one could ever live, lives the whole universe, crying out amidst the calling of the birds.

3

Mònaigh

The sheer physicality of Mònaigh is what strikes you: words die beneath the mountains, thoughts diminish by the sea, hopes moderate in the forest and when you finally stand on the shale-strewn mountain top you are a dwarf and the immediate thought of your own smallness and mortality strikes you like a wind and you need to stand firm, feet set apart, braced against the storm if you are ever to descend again to the land of the living and not turn, as tradition has it, into a bird's feather carried by the wild eagles as the straw of a nest to the rocky faces where the world ends, sharp, like a sheer-cliff face, into the western waters.

The first wanderer to describe Mònaigh was the Roman writer Flavius, who described the island in 200BC: *Terra quoque fortis, et progressus difficilis et laboriosus. Est namque regio quodammodo promontoria. Qudammodo depressa sive plana. Impertansibiles quidem equitibus nisi percaupis in locis, et tum propter in eis continuos nives, excepto solum estatis tempore, perdurantes, tum propter altissimarum preruptos rupium scopulus, tum propter eorum medio concavitates profundas peditibus extant vix meabiles. Quorum vero moncium circa radices nemora sunt ingencia, cervis, damulis aliisque feris silvestribus,*

15

diversi generis et bestiis. Fontes autem ex declivis moncium jugis et collibus nonnulli prorumpentes ebulliunt, et inter ripas ad ima florigeras quam dulci sonite rivulis scaturiunt cristallinis. 'The island land is rugged and progress on it must be difficult and laborious. For this is a region that is partly mountainous and partly lying low or flat. The mountains appear impenetrable except in a few jagged places where the high snow separates above the sheer rock faces of the very high crags, which then plunge down into deep gullies between the ravines. Around the bases of these mountains there are great forests full of stags, fallow deer and other wild animals and beasts of various kinds. Springs also bubble up and burst out from the steeply sloping mountain sides and hills, and they gurgle with a very sweet sound in crystalline rivulets between their banks, which are covered at their edges with flowers.'

Nearer to our own time, the famous English traveller Edmund Burt, writing in the late 1720s, was no less awestruck: 'I have often heard it said by my countrymen, that they verily believed, if an inhabitant of the south of England were to be brought blindfold into some narrow, rocky hollow here, enclosed with these horrid prospects, and there to have his bandage taken off, he would be ready to die with fear, as thinking it impossible he should ever get out to return to his native country.'

These, and a thousand and one other quotes, could of course be interspersed with ten times as many which describe the inhabitants of Mònaigh and elsewhere in the archipelago, as – to quote just one such account (John of

Fordoun's Chronicle of the Scottish Nation, c 1380) – 'a savage and untamed people, rude and independent, given to rapine, lazy, of a docile and warm-disposition, comely in person but unsightly in dress, hostile to the English people and language and – owing to diversity of speech – even to their own nation, and exceedingly cruel.'

Though even that doesn't quite match this masterpiece about the inhabitants of Mònaigh:

How the first Helandman of God was maid
Of ane Horss Turd in Argylle, it is said

God and Sanct Petir was gangand be the way
Heiche up in Ardgyle quhair that gait lay.
Sanct Petir said to God, in a sport word,
"Can you nocht mak a heilandman of this horss turd?"
God turned owre the horss turd with his pykit staff
And up start a helandman blak as ony draff

All that, now, is mere intellectual sud, like the froth left by the receding tide, like the urine stains which cannot be removed from the enamel over which you absently whistle as you piss.

No contemporary traveller to Mònaigh is remotely conscious of these things as she (or he) arrives by car on the ferry and sweep through the eucalyptus-lined avenue which IMG International – formerly Caledonian MacBrayne – have installed to welcome the visitors as they drive from the port terminal to the Tourist Information Point which sits prettily in the sculptured garden, which then leads into the now publicly-owned, once-ancestral, castle.

As a conscious choice, the sculptures are all non-indigenous while the trees and plinths against which they rest and upon which they lean are all native. The sculptures are all open, with hollow innards, and all face outwards towards the seas from which they were made: a hand-crafted enormous marble shell from northern Italy; a long wooden spear (which when you get nearer you suddenly realise is actually made of polished glass, reflecting your own distorted image on the spear-head) from Angola; and – from Iceland – what looks at first like a spouting geyser but in actual fact is a frozen fountain made out of infinitesmal shards of rounded, glazed glass.

In very many ways Mònaigh is the most vibrant of all the island communities. With a population of 8000, and rising, it is almost the most populous, but it is certainly the one where unemployment is least (less than 1.5%), where most new industries are begun, and survive, and where tourism is most successful. Critically, it is the place where the young local people choose to stay, where the young international backpackers choose to come to, and the place, which is fast earning itself the reputation as the Festival centre of the west, even though some of the tabloids have dubbed it the Teuchtar Ibiza.

Certainly on any evening between May and September when you walk along the seafront of the main town, Rockbay – merely a bastardized version of the original name *Roc a' Bhàigh,* which means wrinkled or curled bay – you could be mistaken (at least when it is dry and sunny, which it increasingly is as a consequence of global warming) for thinking you were actually in Corfu or the Bay of Naples or in any one of those thousand and one small vivacious Mediterranean ports. As in these ports, local oysters and scallops are on sale in Rockbay, and at every second seafront cafe you can see or hear a youngster strumming a guitar, or playing a fiddle, or squeezing an accordion, or blowing the pipes or singing Gaelic reels which go on and on, like the kiss or sex you always dreamed of as you move on down to the pier itself where the fishermen are fresh-landing their new-found catch.

Not surprisingly, drugs have entered the scene, though they are not a major problem: there are the usual victims, found overdosed down by the old castle walls, but mostly it is the soft haze of cannabis in the local pubs and the new-found pills and cocaine sniffs in the two former churches which have been converted into clubs, and which glisten yellow and orange and green in the moonlight as the new songs, the profane psalms, throb out.

In the morning, a different people move, as if the revellers of the night before must not be disturbed. Folk move quietly, as if conscious that a child is sleeping in the next room, tousled and fair with the sun shining through on to his tiny palm. Men with dogs gather the morning paper, and a woman with a bag of rolls walks down by the quay, and those beautiful young women – how can there be so many of them? – all dressed for work stand at the bus queue, poised and elegant and free.

You are conscious you don't belong to this place, even though you live next door: here is a finer reality which is rather like London, or at least like the London (the Hampstead or Chelsea) you imagined before you reached London and ended up eternally on that number 79 bus to Hackney. Don't you remember how hot it was in those summer days, and the way – no matter how hard you tried, and no matter how you sprayed yourself – the trickle which turned into a flowing stream would begin under your shirt right there in the hollow of your arm-pit and how you eventually burst out sweating all over, until you wanted to scream?

These girls – and for that matter these young men – don't appear to sweat. Maybe it's your age, or your gender, or your religion, or your background, which causes you this discomfort. See how beautiful it all is, and suddenly you remember how beautiful it all was that July morning in London when the suicide back-packers walked among the crowd. Did they sweat? And if so, with what? With anguish – despair – hope – excitement – fear? Maybe just with the mere physical effort of carrying all that death upon their shoulders?

But perhaps they didn't: maybe they were like the sculptures down by the pier, precise, crafted, hollow and reflective.

You carry all that with you as you spend time in Mònaigh, and it takes you a while to realize that you are a plumed bird lightly shedding your feathers as you fly along. Whether an eagle or a sparrow, it is all the same: by the end of your journey you are bared, and the feathers are gone, God only knows where.

It is, of course, not a conscious plucking. Nor, by any stretch of the imagination, is it any kind of mystic spiritual Celtic experience: after all, each time you sweep round a sharp bend on the bus or in your car and catch a glimpse of the towering hills, you clearly remember that you are a turd, and are glad of it.

But imagine an eagle, all-feathered and beaky-eyed, standing erect and regal on the topmost pinnacle of the most remote crag. Or the sparrow, standing cheekily on the swaying branch in the late March wind. And the huge wings stretch and the chest expands and the talons extend, or the tiny wings flutter and the small chest puffs out and the spindles of the sparrow's legs elongate and off they move, the eagle slicing the universe in half, the sparrow grasping at air.

Imagine – or watch – them flying across the bare skies: the eagle circling, cautious, alert, watchful, predatory, and the sparrow swirling, carefree, swooping, dancing on the thread of a bush.

In London, once, I was the eagle – or the sparrow – and every time I return back home here to my own people on Mònaigh I always again begin as either one or the other and end up undiminished, without a hair on my head, surveying the greatness of it all of which I'm barely a part.

4

Ubhlaigh

One thousand metres away lies the next island in the archipelago: the island called Ubhlaigh.

Etymologists and philologists and linguists have long argued over the derivation of the name. Some argue that it emerges from the Indo-European root word *uvi*, meaning egg-shaped, while others argue that its true origins lie in the crypto-Celtic Welsh word *ouli* meaning a hard-rocked island. Those scholars of Norse inclination point to the obvious *aigh* sound at the end, derived from the Norse word *ey*, simply meaning island, adding the suggestion that the first part comes from a warrior's name – possibly Uvay or Oolay, who may have led the particular Viking tribe which first invaded and conquered the island from whichever group or tribe or clan possessed it at the time.

A further complicated debate has, of course, ensued over that pre-Viking and/or pre-Celtic history, to which various archeologists and archeological institutions and historiographers and cartographers and geographers and scientists and theologians have contributed, ranging from those who argue from fossil evidence that the very first humanoid in Scotland (or at least in old Alba) was found in Ubhlaigh and its vicinity, to those who reason that these very same fossils prove the very opposite, and are mere evidence that reptiles of small human dimension once strayed on to this remote island.

All this – alongside the marvellous bird-life to be found on the sheer cliffs of Ubhlaigh that stretch along the three miles on the west side of the island, and the evidence of a pine-forest of some substance found deep in the peat-soil on the south side, and the relics of ancient wells and crosses of definably pre-Celtic origin – has made Ubhlaigh a living marvel for scholars. The island was readily granted World Heritage Status and has for the past thirty years now been under the aegis and management of Nature Conserve Scotland – previously, of course, better known as Scottish Natural Heritage.

NCS have established a first-class (world-class) research centre on Ubhlaigh to which hundreds of paleologists and entomologists and lepidopterists, as well as anthropologists and environmentalists and retro-sociologists, come each year to observe and study the living and preserved marvels of the island.

The last known silver-tipped butterflies in Western Europe (*Hesperia Common*) are to be found on Ubhlaigh, as is the last known colony of the Slender Scotch Burnet moth, while the wild cliffs and remaining heathland on the west side provide a stunning habitat for the numerous birds which have been extinguished elsewhere – Cory's Shearwater, the rough-legged Buzzard, the Stone Curlew, the Serin and the Ortolan Bunting as well as the great sea-eagle.

The research centre and cliffs and habitats can also, of course, be accessed electronically via the web, so that Ubhlaigh is 'visited' – metaphysically as well as physically – by hundreds of thousands of scholars and researchers as well as surfers and browsers and idlers each year.

The people of Ubhlaigh left the island en-masse in 1945, following the outbreak of a fever, which took all its young people at one stroke. Only the old were spared, presumably because time itself had made them immune to the new disease. No one under sixty survived, and as grandparents buried their children and their children's children and their children's children's children, the weeping was so quiet that you could have mistaken it for utter silence. Instead, it was so deep and mournful that it was beyond all human ken and only the birds and the moths and the butterflies and the insects and the cliffs and the ocean were moved to tears, knowing that their day had come.

As the last child was covered with sand, the rare Melodius Warbler trilled and the new environmental era began.

In old Gaelic mythology, the golden butterfly is held sacred: it is said to be the angel of God come to bear the souls of the dead to heaven. On the day of the great funeral, the golden ascent was seen throughout the western hemisphere: many mistook it for a strange rainbow, many for a flash of lightning. They had good reason, for a butterfly is called *dealan-dè* which means the fire of God.

It was only afterwards that the different speculation began when some smart aleck, idly Googling, discovered that the Ubhlaigh holocaust had happened on the very same day as Hiroshima: the fire of God was perhaps, after all, the fire of Satan reflected across the stratosphere.

None of the old folk who had witnessed the golden butterflies ascending from the machair-land of Ubhlaigh survived long enough to argue against the new mythology, so the uncertainty remains for all visitors to the island: those who work at the research centre tending towards the Satanic definition, the visitors – both physical and electronic – probably equally divided between the old and the new.

There is a story told of a man whose soul returned after wandering through the regions of time and space. The soul alighted on the face of the man in the form of a bee or butterfly, and was about to enter its old home in the body through the pathway of the mouth when a neighbour came along and killed it.

One version of the story says that the body of the man died when his soul was killed; another version says that the body of the man lingered long in the land after the soul was dead, busying itself up and down the earth, carrying the substance of the dead soul in his left hand and the shadow of the withered heart in his right hand.

So with the island of Ubhlaigh, once the home of the solan-goose hunters, perched in their bird-skin moccasins high on the western cliffs, now the international research centre for the birds themselves. It is said that the birds now hunt the travellers, swooping down on them in the lonely gullies to the west, and that the butterflies (or bees) descend in ones and twos on weary travellers on their way home from fossil-research on the shorelines, and that the wild flowers and the insects which grow over and crawl about inside the graves can be heard singing on the evening of an autumn day every ten years, when some forgotten anniversary comes along.

You can become an Honorary Member of the Island of Ubhlaigh Conservation Society by paying an annual subscription of just 30 Euros, for which you receive free access to their marvellous website, a copy of their quarterly illustrated magazine, a beautifully-designed lapel-badge (with the engraving of a kittiwake perched on a cliff) and a 20% reduction in the accommodation quarter of the research centre should you ever manage to visit the island in person.

Ubhlaigh tradition says that there was never a Yellow Butterfly (*An Dealan Buidhe*) on earth until Christ came forth from death and rose up from the tomb. The true Yellow Butterfly, they say, came out of the Holy Tomb, and that Yellow Butterfly spread throughout the world. The true Yellow Butterfly, this tradition asserts, was never seen except among good people.

All efforts to re-introduce this indigenous species to Ubhlaigh have, so far, failed though rumour has it that a light yellow thing was seen briefly fluttering over the highest mountain on the island, Beinn na Sgrath, only last week, as a jet airline passed high overhead.

5

Colathaigh

The people of Colathaigh were always considered eccentric, even by their own kinsfolk and neighbours.

Ritual and practice and tradition and superstition were one thing, but the Colathaighich, as they were known, were considered to take it to extremes. Not only did they observe the Sabbath completely – which of course was Biblical – but they did so sun-wise which, of course, was as pagan as you can have it.

In other words, what they did on Sunday, and, for that matter, every day of the week, was always done moving from left to right on the meridian, or from east to west on the compass. Not that they had, or needed, any physical compass. The long practice of centuries had genetically imbued the population of Colathaigh with an invisible internal compass which gave them the instant ability to tell, with absolute precision, the finite – or infinite – difference between where they stood and where they might stand in a moment, if they only happened to take a single step to the right.

Sunday, of course, was easiest for it was the day they physically moved least, spending it in prayer moving eastwards until – at least on the infinite summer days – they were back where they began, at the hearth, praising God for the spark which had kindled into fire and lasted the entire 24 hours.

The other days were challenging, but as with all great and difficult things, an external observer would not have known how difficult and complicated and orchestrated it all was. Things moved with such an easy gait that the extraordinary had become normal, the miraculous natural.

Fishermen hauled marvellous catches as they followed the sun, while the women washed the blankets in Abhainn Cholaigh as the first rays of the morning sprayed the water, till the tweed covers lay drying on the rocks on the other side of the leaping river, stroked to sleep by the setting evening sun.

Deiseil it was called – 'sun-wise', with the double meaning 'ready'. So to move *deiseil* was not just to move westwards or right with the sun, but also to be alert and ready.

That tradition, of course, went back as far as pagan sun worship, although the indigenous people of Colathaigh were always careful to distinguish between pagan roots and pagan worship. *Tha aon fhear ag aithneachadh, 's am fear eile ag adhradh* – 'One acknowledges, the other worships' they would say, clearly indicating that they were acknowledging, but not worshipping, the sun's power and presence. *Tha feum againn oirre, ach tha fhios againn cuideachd nach do rinn i i fhèin* – 'We live by the sun' they said, 'but we know she was not self-created.'

As with all normalized behavior, very little of this is noticeable or obvious. The people don't move in groups or hordes as they do at football matches or at evangelical rallies. Rather, they move slowly and naturally – alone, ploughing sun-wise with a horse, or in twos as they go off to gather berries, or in threes or fours as they walk to church, or in bands of seven or eight, carrying footballs or tennis-rackets or their i-pods or their mobiles as they move clockwise towards the public playing fields.

They don't have shaven heads, like the Moonies, or nose-rings like the Goths, or rucksacks like the terrorists but are as varied and natural (if that's the word) as any crowd on the King's Road, or on the Oban Esplanade or outside the San Siro in Milan. They have become one with themselves, as they move sunwise.

What has shocked and disturbed Colathaigh in more recent times, however, has been the emergence of a new practice among the indigenous people, which is kind of connected with its past but bears no resemblance to it either. As with all heresies and sects, it has a grain of truth or tradition behind it, but has veered off into a new and dangerous orthodoxy, in danger of blinding the people – especially, in Colathaigh's case, the young, who have become its most ardent adherents – and reducing the practices and culture of the island to disdain and ridicule.

This is the new habit of not just walking sun-wise, but also of never walking or stepping or even looking backwards. The new sect – and no one knows where it all really began and whether there is an official or even

31

quasi-official organization behind it – emerged quickly and almost accidentally, it seems. One day a youngster or two refused to step back in the middle of a running stream and instead leapt forwards. It seems that from that tiny, haphazard beginning a whole new practice has emerged where those who step backwards, or glance backwards, are tut-tutted, frowned upon, disapproved of, even shunned and excommunicated from the company.

In more recent times there has been underground talk of punishment-beatings connected with the backward glance, with rumours ranging from a physical thrashing around the ears for any untoward reference to history, to knee-capping and being thrown off the high Colathaigh cliffs for actually taking a step back, even if a bull or a horse or a high-speed vehicle is rushing towards you.

At first, the elders tried to dissuade the young from the practice of forever veering forwards, no matter the danger or circumstances, but their threats and warning fell on deaf ears. 'Who are you to tell us how to behave?' they said. 'Haven't you yourselves spent hundreds of years perfecting the practice of moving sun-wise? Isn't our moving sun-wise, but constantly forward, but a modernization – or indeed, perfection – of your very own practices?'

The elders preached to them about caution and foresight and the crucial benefits of hindsight and the permanent and increasing need to be aware of what is behind as well as what is ahead, and about the value of history and language and tradition and culture. But the young responded that they were creating their own history and culture, and that looking back was essentially a conservative ideology which halted progress, or at least the pace and direction of that progress.

'Doesn't the same argument apply to your own long-established practices?' they argued. 'Wouldn't you – wouldn't we – all have been better off, by virtue of that argument, moving anti-clockwise as well as clock-wise, the left as well as to the right, to the east as well as to the west? Isn't there as much wisdom moving anti-sunwise as there is sun-wise? Does the moon not bring its own knowledge like the sun, is the left not as good as the right, the east as judicious as the west?'

Some of them, who had been away at university, lucidly argued that the elders had been far too ethnocentric, and cogently pointed out that other cultures, other tribes, others nations and other islands in other archipelagos had utterly different systems, without damage. They reminded them of the tremendously successful system in the United States of Amnesia where the more you forgot the further you progressed and were rewarded.

Their leader, a young man called Caleb, quoted extensively from Frazer's Golden Bough with a litany of names and tribes which had based themselves on the practice of *tuathail* (moving anti-clockwise, from east to west) as opposed to the Colathaighichs' *deiseil*. 'Satanic' and 'anti-Christian' he heard some of the old men and women mutter, but he was smart enough too to quote scripture itself back at them: 'Does not the moon as well as the sun belong to Him? Is he not Lord of the darkness as well as of light, of east as well as of west, of north as well as of south?'

Besides, the new practice was established not through philosophical discussion or reasoned debate but through usage and peer-pressure. Once Caleb led the way – was he not the most handsome male on the island as well as the most well educated? – those who had admired him from youth followed fervently in his footsteps, forever moving forward clockwise.

Well it could be worse, you could hear the older people think. They could have decided not to move sun-wise at all. They could have chosen to do away with the old practices, the old ways altogether. They could have elected to abandon and forsake all known tradition, as all the other islands had, leaving only the old to cling on to the ancient ways, like an abandoned rosary bead.

But they hadn't, and that was to be welcomed. Despite the pressures of the age, despite the vast reading that Caleb had done, despite the amount of time the young spent on their mobile phones and trawling the internet, despite their mobility and their agility, their cars and motorbikes and speed-boats, rather than ditch the old ways they had decided to adjust and add to them, and surely that was to be admired?

One by one, and bit by bit, gradually and over time, the old began to join in the new practice too. First of all the great elder Solar and his esteemed wife Sonas, who began to refuse to balk at all obstacles, who began to refuse to look back to see how much distance they'd covered, and who increasingly rebuked each other if either made any reference to last year or last month or last week or the day before or even the minute before.

'Forward! Forward!' Solar would say, and Solas would shamefacedly look down, having lapsed for a moment into reverie, remembering the particular way in which the sun had slanted over the cliffs the last time they had crossed the river, or the way in which he had once gently taken her in his arms to carry her over the flowing river through which she now stumbled on her knees.

Naturally, the new system required control and order. To be fair to Caleb and his followers, they tried to be relaxed and liberal about that in the beginning, preferring to see a loose *laissez-faire* indigenous structure develop. But it soon became very clear that road led to deviance, disobedience and chaos. So a formal Forward Committee was established, with Caleb as Chairperson and Solar as Vice-chair and a group of what basically became Caleb's young hench-men acting as guardians of the Forward Movement.

Walking or running or driving forward anti-clockwise was the easiest issue, of course. It soon became abundantly clear if an old woman hesitated at a stile, or if a young woman reversed in a car park, or if someone returned home to gather something they'd forgotten. Clear notices were erected forbidding going back. All mirrors were removed from cars and houses and handbags. The reverse gears were disabled in all buses and boats and tractors and trains.

The much more difficult betrayal of the movement to detect was internal: the remembered moment, the long kiss under the moonlight, the tragedy of the younger son's death, the day the great herring fleet came sailing home laden with all the fish in the ocean, that morning Solar had first glimpsed Solas as she stood bathing naked under the waterfall of *Tòrr nan Eas*.

Institutionally, these backward-looking things were well established, so it was simple enough to dis-establish them officially. All history books were burned, all public statues that were dated were torn down, all the songs and stories and myths that were time-specific were erased, so that only those things which were eternally contemporary and dateless, remained.

This effort to create history as it was being made was, of course, doomed to failure. Not because people resisted – which they didn't, at least consciously – but because the logical extension was constant dissolution and erasure. The local school and the local church and the local organizations all officially adopted the new policy, with zeal and rigour and fervour, but it still failed. Fragments of remembered and imagined history would remain, as if taught into the genes – the Flood and the Ark of the Covenant and that time the soldiers sought help after the Battle of Culloden. When was that anyway – 1746? The new policy failed because it meant death. To erase memory was to erase themselves.

So the rope grew tighter. Ancient history – lets say 2000 years ago – was marginally easier to forget (at least for the young) than 200 years ago, or 200 days ago, or 200 hours ago, or 200 seconds ago. They all understood that, and one afternoon one of them spoke it out: 'But if yesterday is forbidden, then surely the same principle should apply to this morning – that too should be erased.' And having spoken that out, the same was spoken for the previous hour, the previous minute, the previous second, and again they all agreed that looking back, even one second, was a compromise with the past which could not be tolerated, a concession which could not be made. For you never knew what it might lead to ... you know, the first step on the slippery slope, give an inch and take a mile, the thin edge of the wedge ... that sort of thing.

'If remembering the last second is valid,' said Gronski, who was Caleb's right-hand man, 'then our whole move-ment is in jeopardy. If Forward means anything, surely it means forward! If the last second is valid so, by extension, is the last minute or hour or decade or century or millennium. If it isn't, then let's hold fast to that principle, without concession, without compromise, without stum-bling, without mercy.'

He was instinctively almost given a round of applause until those who moved their hands remembered (dangerous word!) that it was forbidden to clap what had just happened – it had gone forever. You could only applaud or praise or celebrate or, for that matter, remember the thing as it was actually happening.

And of course it was the island fool who pointed this out, who finally pointed and said – hey, but the Emperor's stark naked! 'Doesn't that mean' he said, 'that we should all just kill ourselves, for our lives are already past?'

They resisted this, of course, pointing out that so much was to come – this evening and tomorrow and the day after and the day after tomorrow and the day after the day after and so on and so forth. 'Don't we have dreams and hopes and plans and proposals and ambitions?' said Caleb. 'Tactics and strategies and devices and campaigns that will move us unceasingly forward, fired by our ideas, inspired by our longings, moved along by the ceaseless tide of our own forward steps, unhindered by the baggage of the past, unimpaired by the memories of both success and failure, liberated from the tethering-ropes of history and practice and superstition and custom, unchained from the fear of the past ...' And the applause, because it was contemporary and continuous, became part of the words as the words themselves became part of the on-going applause.

So they march on in Colathaigh to this very day and this very moment. Round and round in endless circles, sun-wise, stepping forward into a history which has no past because those who make it choose not to remember the moment even of its making in the effort to stay true to a forgotten argument which has neither past nor future.

6

Giuthasaigh

The sixth island in the archipelago has the most southerly aspect and in more recent years has been especially favoured with wind-farms.

As a consequence, the local inhabitants have become rich beyond their wildest expectations and have resorted – naturally – to all the excesses that go with sudden riches, from solid-gold bathtubs to annual excursions to Las Vegas to spend small fractions – millions – of their endless wealth.

Like all fortunes, however, it did not come easily or without struggle. Though the islands bear the full range of religions, the residents of Giuthasaigh have enough of the Calvinist or at least the Protestant work ethic running through their veins to appreciate that luck is earned, and that while grace is given its usage is also blessed.

So while every other island community was arguing vehemently over the merits and de-merits of wind-farms, the good people of Giuthasaigh invited the prospectors and developers and multi-nationals, and their attendant politicians and civil servants, with open and extended arms.

While the residents of nearby Griasabhagh and Siamarbhagh and Stialabhaigh held contentious public-meetings and called in consultants to assess the environmental damage that might be caused by the large-scale wind-farms, the wise people of Giuthasaigh held cèilidhs for them in which bankers danced the long night away, in which the financiers were regaled with the best of the local beverage and in which the prospectors and civil-servants and politicians, both local and national, were promised a share in the investment (and therefore in the profits) that would ensue. It was not quite Whisky Galore, but the same blithe principle applied.

On Griasabhagh the wind-farm development was excluded on the grounds that it would severely damage the extant black-throated seagull population, which was the last known of its kind in the western archipelago. On Siamarbhagh, which consisted of one old indigenous family (*Clann Ruairidh*) and half-a-dozen summer homes, one of which happened to belong to the influential Channel Six broadcaster Jeremy Jacobs, the developers were frightened off by the adverse publicity, while the Stialabhagh protestors objected that wind-farms on their island would seriously harm the burgeoning tourist industry on which they had become increasingly dependent.

Either through indolence or indifference – or perhaps even through vision – the people of Giuthasaigh had none of these difficulties. They couldn't care less whether tourists visited or not; all kinds of black-throated, as well as red-throated, seagulls they took to be pests, and the last TV personality who had tried to purchase a summer-home on the island had ridden off in a fast-boat in the middle of the night following yet another wild booze-up by the locals down the bottom of his garden.

'Ah!' said Archie who, by general definition, was the leader of the Giuthasaigh community by virtue of having sailed twice round the world in the Merchant Navy. 'I see in the West Highland Free Press that everybody these days is having a community buy-out.'

So Archie and his deputy, Mòrag Mhòr (just to keep the gender balance right) were dispatched by first boat to Inverness to make the case for the community buy-out of Giuthasaigh. It was much simpler than expected. The political conditions were absolutely right: the incumbent Labour government were keen on seeing local communities taking ownership of their land, and within the month – following an official visit from officials and political leaders – Giuthasaigh belonged to the people.

There were strings attached, of course: they couldn't just sell it on at a profit to any Tom, Dick or Rebecca who came along, and if any developments were to take place the original funding bodies were to be fully informed and – naturally – given their due return for their money.

The smart move by the residents of Giuthasaigh was to appoint Lucy Stone, a graduate in Economics, as their first Chief Development Officer. Lucy had moved to the island some five years previously when she'd married Archie's son, Lauchlan, a local fisherman. She was the ideal candidate for the job, and within the first twelve months had managed to pay off the initial loan received from government, mostly just by adding a 12% levy on to all non-local fish landings at the new pier. Moreover, she managed to write an obscure legal clause into the new ownership agreement, approved by majority vote at a public meeting. This gave complete authority to the islanders themselves to do with the island as they pleased, without the approval of government, and without any percentage taken by them (tax apart, of course) of the profits.

So when the red-throated seagull watchers of Griasabhagh, and the holiday-cottage owners of Siamarbhagh, and the tourist-dependent population of Stialabhagh rejected the overtures of the wind-farm companies, the good people of Giuthasaigh were set fair for fame and fortune.

'Fuck the environment' was the chant in the local pub, the Solan Goose. And 'fat lot of good birds and wildlife have done for us' the chant by the firesides, and 'no-one can live on fresh air and dreams' the chant among the young, as turbine after turbine, and contractor after contractor, and JCB after JCB, and truncheons of steel after truncheons of steel rolled off in ever-growing succession from the ferry and, increasingly, from private barges that swept backwards and forwards between the mainland and the island, and dangled from helicopters which brought in tons of iron and bolts and soldering materials and welding equipment and personnel to the very tops of the island's five peaks.

It took years to claw out the hillsides and build the access roads required to the separate locations. During those years Giuthasaigh resembled a vast construction site, or a vast rubbish dump, or perhaps the far side of Mars, bare and pitted and pocked and scarred, as seen in those famous photographs taken by the doomed mission Columbia.

'But it will be worth it in the end' you could hear Archie say daily as he stood by his bay window, binoculars focused on the ever-expanding wheels in the sky. 'It will all be worth it in the end – mark my words', and he would remember how the Golden Gate Bridge glittered in the evening sun that first time he'd sailed under it – now then, was it with a cargo of bricks or oil, he wondered?

Strangers came to the island, of course: digger-drivers and lorry-drivers and JCB-drivers and men who hung high on pylons of steel next to the sun, wiring the wind to the brand-new mills, and those who dug the trenches, some more than a thousand feet deep, and bored to the very heart of the earth, then rolled down thin electronic tubes which would carry the seismic waves of the earth's bowels instantly up to the control panel above ground. Alongside these hunter-gatherers came the planners and the financiers and the accountants and the paymasters in their suits and private yachts and – of course – those who provided for their every need, from the resident cook to the peripatetic prostitute.

But as with the Pyramids themselves, there comes a day when the final brick is laid and the last slave is unleashed, and there came the day when the turbines were erect and polished, when the windmills glistened and shone, when the roads were paved and kerbed, when the heather was replaced, when the scars were landscaped and decorated and the wind-farms began rolling, catching the enormous wind coming in from off the Atlantic and turning it into kilowatts of electricity, into euros and dollars.

The sub-sea cable took the harnessed wind, and the receiving power companies subsequently dispatched the agreed amounts by individual bank credit to the islanders who replaced the decaying outhouses with summer chalets, who replaced the worn-out fishing boats with a brand-new fleet, who replaced the old cars and tractors with Rolls Royces and Mercedezes.

The gold baths came, and the gilded taps and the diamond-encrusted shoes (they never went as far as diamond-encrusted wellies), while the old sheep-fanks and the cattle-barns and the field where the wild horses once stood were transformed variously into a cycle-track, an adventure-park, and a place where the leisure-centre, with its chutes and slides, its tennis and squash courts, resounded to the whoops and cries of delighted children as they flew through the darkened space into the chlorined water.

But when the evening comes, and the leisure-centre staff go home, and later on when the pubs and the clubs and the casino and the late-night brothel down by the pier, at *Rubh nan Àird* close, they say a keening sound is heard throughout the island which neither the jangle of the gold bracelets nor the soft whine of the revolving steel windmills quite manage to drown. They say that it is like the sound of a child crying, the whimper that emerges when the major grief and anger has gone, and only the quiet sobbing is left, like drifting seaweed between the high tides.

7

Fleadaigh

Is the island where all the local people have turned into stone, or wood, or stream.

Once upon a time, of course, it was the other way round: every tree you approached was a human being, every stream you crossed cried out, every stone you picked or threw would deliver a sermon or a song or a tale, in the old, long way.

In those days, when you arrived by boat on the island you were waved to while still a long way off by the ancient yew tree which had somehow managed to wrap itself round the shrapnel of rock upon which the pier life-buoys were hooked. As you drew nearer it was Duncan the Master Mariner, who had already seen two world wars and whose sole pastime now was to stand on the pier each time a ferry arrived in the ardent hope that this time, surely, it was John or young Duncan come back home.

Off the ferry, the smithy was on the right hand side as you climbed the brae and the sparks from the furnace spoke to you. Listen to us, they said, for we have come out of peat and coal and iron – out of the softest and sweetest, out of the darkest and hardest things on and under the earth – and have been transformed into these lacy fiery fragments.

Watch us, they said, as we fly into life from the anvil, red-hot and burning, and as we fall how we become light and bright and airy and how we dissolve into the dust and ash that crumble at the smithy's feet.

You looked up and it wasn't the sparks speaking at all, but the smithy himself – a fellow by the name of Smith (*Mac a' Ghobhainn*), not surprisingly. His language was old and mostly incomprehensible, the rich, thick words falling like sparkling fragments at your feet as you listened and tried to understand: now there's a word – *gròibleach* (long-nailed, or having talons) – and there's another – *dà-bheathach* (amphibious) – and there's another – *tarbh-dallaig* (blue shark). But there are too many that you cannot understand or grasp the meaning of, and down they descend into ashes in your ears.

You would walk up towards the old village, past the schoolmaster's house and past the manse and past the post-office and shop, and the slightly-rising breeze would whisper to you that bad weather was coming in, until you realised that it was old Flora in her roadside cottage telling you that the barometer was falling and that rain was imminent. The raven on the telegraph-pole at the corner would sing a song until you realised it was old Seumas inside the byre singing to himself, and the little waterfall at the top of the brae would ask you your business until you realised it was a young girl sitting by the fall asking nonchalantly where you were going.

Inside these old houses – for sometimes you had to go in there, on errands from your parents – the darkness spoke and cajoled and moved and threatened. 'How are they back home?' it would ask. 'And is your poor Auntie Peggy still unwell?' or 'Will you need to go straight back on the next ferry', and the darkness turned out, later, to have been your mother's aunt or your father's grand-aunt or some unspecified person who owed a kindness for a kindness done a very long time ago.

You emerged, carrying a pail of milk, or a bucket of butter, or jars of jam, made and distributed by women out of the darkness and out of the loud silence.

But that – that, of course, was in the old days, a long, long time ago, when thatch spoke or when rook warned or when tree moved.

Now, as I say, the opposite is true. Duncan is there sure enough, down by the pier, but as soon as you speak to him he turns into a yew tree, and the old smithy is there (though converted into a coffee-house) but when you address the owner it's your own words that rise and fall like ash to the floor. And as you walk through the village the voices are clear and distinct and perfectly understandable and English, while the little girl by the waterfall has been taken away by the police for her own safety, though the abuse of what was once innocent continues despite the new sexual obsessions.

Above and beyond the village, through the woods and trees, way past the ancient well and the old iron-works, you finally reach the vantage-point where you can look back and see the whole island stretched before you, out into the firth which reaches out towards the next island which leans westwards on its elbow at the outer limits of the archipelago.

Today, the sea is calm and aquamarine, like the liquid eyes of that girl you saw for a brief moment once in Casablanca as she darted suddenly out of a shop doorway and disappeared forever into the crowd. Far above, the clouds are small and white and opaque, like memory itself before it crushes you, turning everything into a downpour until the streams overflow and the dams burst and the fields flood.

You realize that you are standing soaking wet in the actual pouring rain, which came so suddenly and so unexpectedly, like the voice of the dead or like the death of your father. And equally as quickly it ceases, the sun streams through and the steam begins to rise from your jacket which you suddenly become conscious of being heavy and wet and warm. Your finger goes through the familiar hook and you sling it over your shoulder as you travel back down hill, past the old iron-works and the ancient well, through the woods and the trees, into and beyond the village, on to this page.

You comprehend that the jacket is made of wool yet bears the label Harris Tweed, just as you acknowledge that the voices you heard all along were your own. Nothing is silent, except for yourself, and you understand that the stones and the woods and the trees only told what you knew already. It was you who gave them speech and language, just as it was you who gave them silence and strangeness. Their muteness, like their eloquence, is your own, and their dumbness, like their song, was once yours.

8

Beurla

The Island of Beurla is where all of the old ways and all of the old language have been forsaken because a tall man came in 1872 and told the natives that it was now forbidden to speak in their own tongue.

Half said, 'Yes, yes' and the other half dissented but some of them were beaten, some of them exiled, and the rest paid to abandon their language.

'Have you come on your own?' a young man asked the tall man, thinking for a moment that he would watch where the tall man went, who he talked with and what he did, and that then, in the shade of the night, he would kill him. 'Oh no' said the tall man, 'No, I haven't come on my own. Some of your people here probably met my father and my father's father.'

And some of the island elders nodded their heads sagely, agreeing that they had seen his likeness, his forebears before.

'You're very like your father' one of the wizened ones said and the tall man smiled, pleased to have been recognized by his father's angular features.

'And your grandfather' said the wizened one's wife. 'He was a fine man. A gentleman. A man of great manners' and the tall thin one smiled again, well pleased.

'And have you got children?' the old wizened one's wife continued. 'And a wife?' and the tall thin one smiled and said 'Madam – where I come from we don't have a wife. We have wives. So therefore I have many children, and as many grand-children again and again as many great and great-great-grandchildren.'

'Lovely' said the people, spontaneously bursting into a round of applause, 'new generations to come. More young people for our community. Young men who will sail the boats. Young women to marry. And are they pretty?'

'Yes' smiled the tall man, being led into the elder's house. 'Yes, they are very pretty.'

The people gathered round the tiny windows and the tiny door to try and catch a glimpse of the stranger, but the small smoky house was so crowded that they couldn't see him. That, however, didn't deter them, for they were delighted to listen to him, hearing his strange, marvellous words floating out through the holes in the thatch. 'Dev-El-Op-Ment' the people shyly whispered to one another, hearing the word pouring out of the esteemed visitor's mouth. 'Pro-Gress' they lisped to one another as if the words were sacred and magical, which they were.

Unlike them, the tall man was more concerned about what he called the future than about what had already happened. 'Don't concern yourselves with these things' he said. 'After all, of what interest is that which has already happened? You know that already. What you need to concern yourselves with are the things that have not happened yet, the things that are to come.'

Of course they had heard all that before: didn't they hear it every Sabbath from the pulpit, and wasn't what they completely believed already, and wasn't that what they already based their lives upon? This tall handsome stranger who spoke so well was only, after all, confirming what they already knew and believed.

So the stranger stayed on the island for a very long time, teaching from house to house. He taught them that $1+1 = 2$ and that the cat always sat on the mat and that if you wrote a thing called A you pronounced it 'Eh' and not 'Ah', and he told them many marvellous tales about things called the Spanish Armada and the House of Tudor and the Wars of the Roses, which all sounded terribly exciting and far stranger than the stories they had about Cuchullain and Brian Boru and Mac Iain 'ic Sheumais, which he told them were 'myths' though most of them could never pronounce the word properly and called it 'mys'.

Now when I say that the stranger stayed on the island for a very long time, I don't mean to imply that he did all this marvellous work on his own: that would have been too much even for a tall man of his perspicacity, zeal and intelligence. Not only did he bring his wives and his children and his children's children with him to help with the work, but also even more wisely he married several other local wives who, of course, bred his own indigenous children.

'This is my wife' he said to the gathered natives when a beautiful fair-haired woman sailed in one day with a basket of fruits over one arm and a dazzling parasol in the other.

'Her name is 1914', and the natives bowed down before her glory. 'And this is my eldest son' he then said, when a beautifully dressed man with perfectly-manicured hands and a perfectly balanced goatee-beard came floating down from an airship. 'His name is Electricity'. And of course you can probably guess all the names and appearances of all the other dazzling wives and children, ranging from 'Television' (which the natives softly pronounced as *Telefisean*) to 'Shame'.

The islanders, of course, were not fooled by any of this: certainly some were dazzled by the marvels, and some believed, and some were bought, and some were forced, but all were persuaded. His local wives were mostly from the aristocracy, the daughters and grandaughters of the chiefs who had already made peace treaties and agreements with the tall thin man's great-great-grandfather, at Iona in 1509. But there were some dragged up from the byre to become handmaidens and others bought out of the slavery of their poverty to become genteel ladies at the great table.

And some of their sons and their son's sons became schoolmasters and generals and taught others to become the same, and who – after all – can blame them?

After a while the tall man became taller, or shorter, according to whom you listened to. Some said that he had been a stranger, some a friend. Some said that, like the Loch Ness Monster, he had never existed while others argued that of course he had – but had only stayed a night or a day or a week or a month or a year or a century, they couldn't quite remember which. Others said that he had never left and would whip out their mobile phones or their grand-children or their fictions and say – 'Look – here are his grand-children!'

But when you now visit this island, the one they still call Beurla, the question is never raised. Whether the tall thin man ever existed is as irrelevant as whether the King of Egypt once wore a feathered hat or whether Fionn actually killed and ate the eight wild pigs after the one chase. He has become so important – or so irrelevant – that he is taken for granted. He has eaten the grass and swallowed the seas and crushed the stones on the shore and drunk the lochs of the island so that with every bite you eat or every sip that you drink or every step that you take you become the tall thin man who has now become so tall as to be unseen and so thin as to be invisible.

When you ask the people if they know anything about him or if they've seen him (surely there must be some ancient memories of him, surely the remnants of some antique Victorian school stand?) they shake their heads and say that someone took him away. 'Who?' you ask. 'Oh – some stranger' they say. 'A tall thin man who came with a crane and broke the old schoolhouse down, and we think he put the crushed stones into the new road that runs across the island over there.'

Always the stranger, always the other from someplace else, always some tall thin man who came and took the cards from our hands and froze the words on our lips and took the goodness out of our music and swept the fire from the centre of the floor and set a searing bonfire in our hearts.

And that tall thin man was always, of course, ourselves; for when we all sat and listened to the story we understood it all perfectly because it was in the stranger's tongue – in other words in our own tongue – and the only thing that really puzzled us was the name of the story itself, the actual name of the island itself, now half-forgotten, just like the tall thin man.

'What does it mean?' we ask, as if a word has precise meaning and as if the word, which we can't understand, when translated, will suddenly acquire that meaning. As if the story has a fixed explanation. As if the word 'Beurla' for example, which can be translated as 'English', will make more sense when, instead of the original *Eilean na Beurla* we use the half-hybrid 'The Island of *Beurla*' or the thin man's terminology 'The Island of English'.

As if, by speaking in our own language, we would suddenly understand 'Island', or 'English', any more than we ever understood anything before the tall thin man, or any of his predecessors or descendants, came to explain them to us.

9

Labhraigh

By far the most interesting island linguistically is the Island of Labhraigh which, through the course of time, has developed an entire speech system based on conversation, or what grammarians used to call the Present Indicative active tense, mood and voice.

What has happened on Labhraigh is that the Present and Future tenses, and the Imperative and Subjunctive moods and the Future voice have not so much been abolished or discarded, but rather have been incorporated into the one tense – the Present – and into the one mood – the Indicative – and into the one voice – the Active.

On the surface of things, this might appear to make their language (or perhaps more appropriately their dialect) simpler, by virtue of having reduced matters. In actual fact it makes it far more complicated, and almost entirely reliant for understanding on inflection, tone, circumstance, intent – on those almost infinite things which are entirely contextual and depend upon mood, facial expression, the lifting or lowering of an eyebrow, left or right or both, and so on and so forth.

In short, when you are conversing with a native of the island of Labhraigh, the conversation is as much a puzzle as a revelation, as much a game as a dialogue, as much a mystery as a communication. And not only because you can't really fully understand or appreciate what they are saying to you – the rules apply both ways, and your feeble attempts to say 'Good morning', for instance, can as easily be understood by them as 'I've just had a bath' (if you happen to lower one shoulder), or even 'Can I sleep with your wife?' (if you happen first to lower one shoulder, then the other).

Much like the language itself, the derivation or origin of this particular usage lies shrouded in mystery, in the lost history of time. Some argue that it was a habit brought in by the survivors from the Spanish galleon *La Santa Maria* which shipwrecked nearby in 1580. Those few who crawled ashore obviously couldn't speak Gaelic, and (perhaps equally obviously, perhaps not) none of the people of Labhraigh could speak Spanish either, so in the developing effort to communicate with one another a kind of visual-verbal patois – a sort of marriage of the Gallic and Gaelic shrugs – emerged which has now left us with this contextualized language.

Others, however, date the linguistic phenomenon to a later period, attributing it – like most other things, it has to be said – to the debacle of Culloden, and especially its horrific aftermath when the Redcoats scoured the area for rebels, burning, pillaging, raping and looting all along the way. It is suggested that when the Redcoats came ashore on Labhraigh (historical evidence, after all, verifies that they even reached as far as St Kilda looking for a bonny Prince whom the natives had never heard of!) the local people –

who knew little or no English either – resorted to cautious, contextualized answers which, utterly dependent upon body-language, could be interpreted any way the Redcoats desired. They left the next morning concluding, of course, that the natives of Labhraigh were – even more so than all the other islanders – indolent, ignorant, and un-communicative. What saved the island from being burned, and the women from being raped, was that the Redcoats – wrongly – assumed that the islanders, despite their ignorance, had done their best to help.

These, of course, are all folk versions of the linguistic phenomenon: the truth, if such exists, no doubt lies along more scientific lines. The more recent philologists and morpholigists (at least those of the post-Zwollfian persua-sion) generally attribute linguistic variation (or deviation, depending on your point of view) to structural, or post-structural, reasons – in other words, much as in biology and entomology, the 'norm' is always relative, and all languages, just like cells, are essentially authentic variants of their own history.

Where initial or individual 'change' begins to take place is always almost impossible to classify. The most that can be said, according to these experts, is that words change – for the usual variety of historic, political, social, cultural and psychological reasons. New 'cool' words enter daily and old obsolete ones die away. But once they enter, they are almost immediately 'normalized' and become part of the gram-matical function and structure of the evolving language.

Thus, they say, the shrug of the shoulders, or the

stretching out of the open palms, or the lift of an eyebrow: like the Carolingian lisp in Spanish, what was once a kingly aberration becomes the common standard.

As with all other languages and dialectical variations, the language used in Labhraigh leads to differing degrees of fluency, and tone, and texture, over which there is constant discussion. Some argue that the north end of the island – being furthest away from the pier and therefore from contamination – is where the purest form of the language is to be found, but even within that configuration further distinctions need to be made. Half of that northern end is Roman Catholic while the other half is Protestant; and of course within that Protestant half there are further sub-divisions and classifications, with most language users and scholars agreeing that the best and purest diction and the richest terminology by far resides with the small and diminishing Free Presbyterian flock whose vocabulary mixes the classical Biblical language of Isaiah and Jeremiah with their own land-based traditions connected with horses, cattle, sheep and goats.

Most users of the language would concede that because of the usual Calvinist reasons (as elsewhere, strict orthodoxy took hold among some of the people from the mid-18th century onwards) this Free Presbyterian stronghold lacks part of the wide and more free-ranging vocabulary – and the bodily gestures that go with it – held by the Catholics, especially when it comes to the much more 'secular' subjects, such as song, tale, story, myth, legend and so on.

It has to be remembered, however, that this discussion generally excludes the fact that most of the scholars, like most of the collectors – and indeed like most of the language learners – tend to go to the remaining Roman Catholic population as a first port of call, mostly because they then don't run the danger of having to attend long endless Sabbath meetings, with the added peril that they might even be converted!

These gradations of language fluency and skill have their class basis too, of course: generally speaking, the more ancient and the 'purer' the language of the bearer is, the more his socio-linguistic status increases. Those few who still carry the original Fingalian tales with them in undistilled form are, of course, top of the anthropological tree, along with the other great tradition-bearers of the old songs, the old ways, the old traditions.

But even that, however, needs some qualification, for in the south end of the island – which is the much more 'developed' end, where the two industrial units lie – these tradition-bearers tend to be increasingly viewed as anachronisms, counter-weights to progress and the image-carriers of a backward culture. There, in the local pub, I have heard these tradition-bearers (those myth-carriers) scathingly referred to as 'fluent liars', which some of them – naturally – would accept as a tremendous compliment! Rather than being high on the social scale these tradition-bearers are – at one end of the island – considered of low esteem and of declining status.

A huge industry has developed round or at least from

these very linguistic issues. The Labhraigh speech-and-body pattern has become an international phenomenon, and although it bears a close enough relationship to the other Celtic languages, has increasingly been recognized as a valid, vital and vibrant part of a modern, 21st century multi-culturalism. In fact, I just lifted the words 'valid, vital and vibrant' from their latest brochure.

Indeed, the Labhraigh speech-and-body pattern has gradually assumed a symbolic function as articulating in one visual-speech community all the diversity and multi-plicity the world has been so brutally stripped of. Ecologists warm to it, as do environmentalists and all other people of sound and healthy mind who recognize that language-stripping is every bit as destructive for the world's environment as the stripping of the Amazonian rainforest, or the destruction of the Hindu Kush plateau. The Labhraigh speech-and body pattern is therefore now part of the official bio-diversity programme acknowledged and supported (financially and otherwise) by the likes of Greenpeace and Friends of the Earth, but even more exciting in recent times has been its official recognition by government itself as an endangered species which needs special help and aid and protection.

It was, of course, tremendously disappointing for the users and supporters of Labhraighese – as it has become officially known – that the disciples of old Bob Geldof did not include this fragile speech-and body community in the on-going G8 campaign and rock concerts. They feel, naturally, part of the impoverishment of the world and would very much have liked to have been officially included in the Make Poverty History campaign, though the more committed members, who've been at it for a long time, have already publicly stated their well-being does not depend upon the disciples of Geldof or Hewson.

But that's by the by, for the island – and therefore its speech-and-body language – is already beginning to thrive. Already twenty-five nursery playgroups operating through Labhraighese are up and running, there are two primary schools on the island teaching the entire curriculum through the speech-and-body language, and several subjects (including of course Art) are on offer in the local High School for those young students who wish to pursue the speech-and-body language to higher levels.

Three of the national universities offer Labhraighese as a Course Option in their Arts Degree, but the most innovative development has, of course, been the establishment of the Labhraighese-Medium College on the island, through which students from all over the world can learn and use the speech-and-body language in a variety of courses, ranging from Hairdressing through the medium of Labhraighese to Creative Writing in and through the body-language.

Hundreds of students join these courses each year. Increasingly, with the use of the internet and distance-learning, a world-wide network of students and learners and graduates is being established who can recognize each other by the half-wink of an eye, perhaps, or – at the much more advanced level (Level Eight and beyond) – by opened mouth suggestion (unspoken) of the half-wink of an eye. Not especially easy through video technology, but most students accept that as one of the extra enjoyable challenges involved in reaching some degree of fluency in this complex language.

The usual campaigns are underway, of course, to establish a Labhraighese digital television channel, though so far the Government has resisted all efforts to adequately fund such a channel, arguing that the bodily (visual) side of the culture is the only one it could fund, and that the matching fund for the linguistic (verbal) side of the language is one that the community itself needs to raise. Preliminary talks have already taken place between the government and community representatives to move towards splitting the language into its distinctly visual and verbal components. The working committee's initial proposals give a tentative welcome to such a division, cogently arguing that double-funding could then conceivably become available through European funding, which would see the specialist development of a radio channel for the verbal side of the language, leaving the television channel to deal with the complex visual/body elements involved.

Opponents, naturally, describe the whole notion as foolish, like trying to separate the salt from the sea, or the veins in the body from the skin. How can you divide that which is indivisible, they argue – how can you distinguish the stars from their effulgence, or the oceans from their wetness?

At the heart of the issue remains the whole question of

the language itself. Beyond the technology and the developments and the courses and the graduates and the prospective media channels, the vexed question of the Present Indicative Active remains. With no verbal structure to differentiate the past from the present or the present from the future or, for that matter the future from the past, the whole language has already entered a plateau of confusion where the communicants are unsure as to whether the world that is being given is living, dead or imagined.

In the Labhraighese dialect, or language, there are no words for 'yesterday' or 'today' or 'tomorrow', as there are no verbal concepts as such for 'was', 'am' or 'will'.

Instead the singular root word *diugh* is used to indicate yesterday, today and tomorrow with a slight almost inaudible (and almost invisible) inflection in the 'u' vowel to suggest whether you are referring to yesterday, today or tomorrow. That inaudible and invisible inflection is, of course, almost impossible to replicate here on paper, but I'll have a go: the first 'u' sound in *diugh* to indicate 'yesterday' sounds like the 'u' you use or hear in the words such as 'you' and 'lieu' and 'pew', while the 'u' sound you use or hear in *diugh* to indicate 'today' has a slightly more 'rounded' sound, almost tending towards an 'o' sound, as for example in the English words 'dew' or 'yew' or 'sew' (this, of course, is all dependent upon accent and so forth as well), while the 'u' sound that is used or heard to indicate the future has a fractionally sharper tone to it, such as in the English words 'new' or 'phew!' or 'Jew'. The important qualification is that these last words need to be pronounced slightly faster than the norm so that a sort of 'iu' sound emerges rather than the usual 'eu' sound.

If this all sounds complicated, I want to stress that part of the complication lies in the inarticulacy of the page itself. Being a supremely oral and corporeal language, the nuances and movements may require musical or visual notation rather than linguistic ones, and the actual physical (as well as metaphysical) reality of Labhraighese itself is – like Newtonian physics – easy enough once it is understood and practised.

The problem, of course, is that the life-source of the language itself is rapidly dissipating: the number of indigenous native-speakers or users of the language is diminishing each year – for every 1000 that die each year, they are 'replaced' by only 300 who are learning the language through the education system – so that the balance between an authentic curved extension of the left forefinger (signifying goodbye) and a half-learned somewhat straightened extension of the left forefinger (signifying hello) is becoming rather fragile.

The older native speakers and some scholars despair, lamenting that 'modern' Labhraighese is but a pale, sickly imitation of the once-rich and vibrant language that they knew. The range has diminished, they say, as has the tone and tempo and actual accuracy of the language, while those who are learning clearly argue that a half-loaf is better than none. *'S fhèarr Labhraighese bhriste, seach Labhraighese na ciste* they say – 'Better Labhraighese badly spoken, than Labhraighese confined to the coffin.'

The encouraging thing is that it all happens in the present tense: with no past and no future, all the arguments, all the discussions, all the disagreements as well as the births and marriages and deaths happen now. Increasingly, as folk are unable to distinguish those miniscule gestures which distinguished the past from the future, all happens now: nobody goes to the shop except now, nobody leaves the island except now, nobody dies except now, except that everyone knows, despite all the clamour, that the now they speak of is already past, or is yet to be.

10

St Eòinean's

As you move north, St Eòinean's becomes the first place which takes on a different bareness: hitherto, the land has been soft and white or elemental and majestic, but even from the air as you fly on, the austerity of St Eòinean's is striking.

Unlike Craolaigh, it is more than a mere lump of rock, and unlike Mònaigh it does not dwarf, and unlike Ubhlaigh, for instance, it does not entice with heath or machairland or fjords. In a sense, it is undistinguished except for its bareness, which is not the bareness of emptiness and nothingness but rather that bareness which tempts and reveals.

It would be too much to compare it to a naked woman (or man, for that matter). Rather, it is the temptation of the veil, or of the gauze, or of that glimpse of bare thigh remembered from a train corridor long years ago.

The most extraordinary story concerns St Ronan who arrived in the western archipelago early in the seventh century. Angus Gunn from Ness on the Island of Lewis was 84 years of age when he told this story, well over a hundred years ago: 'Ronan came to Lewis to convert the people to the Christian faith. He built himself a prayer-house at

Eoropie, but the people were bad and would not give him peace. The men quarreled about everything, and the women quarreled about nothing, and Ronan was distressed and could not say his prayers for their clamour. He prayed to be removed from the people of Eoropie, and immediately an angel came and told him to go down to the *laimrig* – the natural landing rock – where the *cionaran-crò* was waiting for him. Ronan arose and hurried down to the sea-shore shaking the dust of Eoropie off his feet and taking nothing but his *pollaire* (satchel), containing the Book, on his breast. And there, stretched along the rock, was the great *cionaran-crò*, his great eyes shining like two stars of night. Ronan sat on the back of the *cionaran-crò*, and it flew with him over the sea, usually wild as the mountains, now smooth as the plains, and in the twinkling of two eyes reached the remote isle of the ocean.

'When Ronan landed on the island it was full of *"nathair bheumnaich, gribh inich, nathair nimhe, agus leòmhain bheucaich"* (biting adders, talonned griffins, poisonous snakes, and roaring lions). All the beasts of the island fled before the holy Ronan and rushed backwards over the rocks into the sea. And that is how the rocks of the island of Ronaigh are grooved and scratched and lined with the claws and the nails of the unholy creatures. The good Ronan built himself a prayer-house in the island, where he could say his prayers in peace.'

Tradition has it that other manifest adders and griffins and snakes and lions troubled Ronan: deprived of the company of women for so long, it is said that finally he began to cast incestuous eyes on his sister who had accompanied him all the way through the heathen west. She was exiled to the even more remote (uninhabited) island of Sula Sgeir where she starved to death; her skeleton found years later with a crested cormorant found nesting its young in her chest cavity.

Bareness may conceal as much as it may reveal, though when the revelation comes it is, surely, as stark and complete as Beathag's (for that was her name) scavenged chest cavity. Didn't the great MacDiarmid once have a plagiarized poem about the pigeon's skull found on the South Uist machair? All the bones, pure white and dry, and chalky, but perfect, without a crack or a flaw anywhere – and at the back, rising out of the beak, were domes like bubbles of thin bone, almost transparent, where the brain had been that fixed the tilt of the wings.

Or elsewhere, as he put it: the inward gates of a bird are always open. But whether any man's are ajar is doubtful. Except, perhaps, those of the travelling saint.

Think of that quest for holiness: the sea always further, the departing land – the dear green place – never left behind until it disappeared even when the eyes were closed, in prayer – the search for the rock, the reef, the strand, the mound that was pure and uncontaminated. And the knowledge which travelled with you in that boat, the adder of despair, the griffin of unbelief, the snake of desire, the lion of ambition and the certainty that once you got there, to that unpolluted place, there they would be slithering and standing and guffawing and roaring before you, waiting for death: all death.

And there, on the rock with your eyes closed you would take courage: remember how Patrick rid Ireland of all snakes, and how George purged England of all dragons, and how Christ Himself (Ah! Now we have it) how Christ Himself defeated the Devil in the desert, and routed the thieves in the temple, and vanquished death at Calvary and overpowered sin and mortality in the empty tomb! This rock, this outcrop, this island here on the edge of the ocean, on the edge of the earth, in the very centre of the world, in the cavity, the bare cavity of my heart, is the cross and tomb of victory!

And compare that to the other – the same – quest for holiness in the glorious chambers of Chartres and in the dazzling heavenly mansions of Michelangelo's chapel: the rocks of the island grooved and scratched and lined with the claws and the nails of the retreating creatures, and the ceiling of the Sistine grooved and scratched and lined with the plaster-bevels and the iron-styli of the flattened artist advancing towards God.

Did the outstretched finger reach Ronaigh more easily than Rome? No: surely it was the other way round, as the one Adam stretched high on the scaffolding above the Popes and the other Adam, exiled beyond the shade of the garden in the cool of the evening, clambered and scrambled over the precipices to touch, with their own fully outstretched souls, the electric finger which had drawn them in the first place to this abyss – to this sanctuary – scaffolded above the ocean, to this rocky island – this haven – inches from heaven?

St Eòinean's Isle, as it is known, is one of those

sanctuaries which was officially dedicated to a variety of saints in the Middle Ages – to *Naomh Eòinean* (Saint Eòinean, or little Jonathon, or John), one of the hundreds of Celtic saints who came to Scotland from Ireland in the wake of *Colm Cille* (Columba), Moluag, Maolrubha – Ronan, of course – and others.

Little is known about Eòinean himself, and whether he actually ever settled on the Isle which is now named after him, though tradition bears some evidence that he did. There is a well on the island believed to have been blessed by Eòinean in which epileptics were cured, and at least one version of an old prayer giving thanks for an abundance of seaweed makes reference to the intercession of Eòinean, though most other traditions attribute the providence of seaweed (essential for manuring the land and therefore for crops and survival) to either Saint Connan or Saint Patrick:

Thàinig 's gun tàinig feamainn,
Thàinig 's gun tàinig brùchd,
Thàinig buidheag 's thàinig liaghag,
Thàinig biadh mun iadh an stùc.

Thàinig Mìcheal mìl na conail,
Thàinig Brìghde bhìth na ciùin,
Thàinig a' Mhàthair mhìn Mhòire,
'S thàinig Eòinean/Connan/Pàdraig àigh an iùil.

Seaweed has come, and come plentifully,
Red sea-ware has arrived, and plentifully,
Yellow weed and tangle in vast plenty,
Our food has come wrapped in the ocean waves.

Michael the fruitful warrior has come,
Bridget the gentle woman has come,
Mary the mild Mother has arrived,
And the glorious Eòinean/Connan/Patrick has come
    to guide.

It has to be remembered that though many of these Celtic missionaries set down roots and established themselves in particular places, as many again were, as Scripture put it 'aliens and strangers on earth who went about in sheepskins and goatskins, destitute, persecuted and ill-treated – the world was not worthy of them. They wandered in deserts and mountains, and in caves and holes in the ground.' (Hebrews Chapter 11).

The ruins of monastic cells and beehive huts are to be found all over the western archipelago, but apart from a vague scattering of stones within a concave hollow above the sea's edge, no physical evidence remains that St Eòinean stayed for 50 years (as oral tradition has it) on this rocky outpost. Maybe like Enoch, or like the mythic Celtic saint Dreaghan, he was directly transported to heaven on the back of the angel whose ascent was always recognized by the sudden movement of a fountain of rainbow-coloured water rising into the east.

But whether Eòinean ever actually stayed on the isle more than a single prayerful night in a cartographic sense doesn't matter. Following the formal expulsion of the Vikings after Largs in 1263 and the establishing of the Lordship of the Isles he became part of the great theological mapping of the late-13th century when Reginald, First Lord of the Isles accompanied the Bishop of Sodor on the great journey which saw so many ancient Celtic sites re-claimed and re-dedicated to the indigenous saints.

The bareness of the island today is, therefore, full of substance: the tiny gap between the finger of Adam and the finger of God is filled with the awesome history of the whole world and the grand plan which Michelangelo Buonarrotti mapped out for the Sistine Chapel. In the four corners are David And Goliath, and Judith and Holofernes, and The Brazen Serpent and The Death of Haman; along the top are Dephica, Josiah, Isaiah, Esekias, Cumaea, Asa, Daniel, Jesse and Libyca; along the bottom are Joel, Zorababel, Erythraea, Ozias, Ezekiel, Roboam, Persica, Salmon and Jeremiah, with the central panel containing the great themes: The Drunkenness of Noah, The Deluge, The Sacrifice of Isaac, The Temptation and Expulsion, The Creation of Eve, The Creation of Adam, The Separation of Land from Water, the Creation of the Sun, Moon and Plants, and The Separating of the Light from the Darkness; with the two smaller end panels depicting Zechariah and Jonah completing the work.

The awsome glory of Rome is brought to full life on the bare rock of St Eòinean's which no one ever visits – perhaps not even the one whose name belongs to it and who is so highly revered in the mythology of our times.

11

Gearraidh

Gearraidh is conceived of as one island, but is really two, being divided twice a day by the incoming tide when the low-lying strand becomes completely impassable except by boat.

Some argue, of course, that it is the other way round: that Gearraidh is really two islands which become one twice every twenty-four hours when the ocean tide recedes to reveal the sandy isthmus which, like an invisible umbilical cord, connects the two civilizations.

Gearraidh's tidal flows are as complicated as any, taking in cosmology, meteorology, oceanography and micro-climatology. To even begin to appreciate them, you need to know about the cycles of the moon and the sun, the infinitely varying circumstances and conditions affecting what we generally, and vaguely, call 'weather', altered by wind and rain and ocean surface temperatures, by global isobaric and geological conditions, by local environmental usage and alteration, and by a thousand and one other things which we neither know nor understand, or appreciate.

I have before me Bartholomew's Edition of the *Oxford Advanced Atlas* for 1942, for example, and it would take longer to understand a single page of that great atlas than it has taken to begin to appreciate that the underlying, almost invisible, differences between the northern part of Gearraidh and the southern part are as great as the differences between the first page, marked Astronomical Charts, and the very last page which maps New Zealand and the Pacific Isles.

That first page – and maybe our astronomical knowledge has magnified the generations since? – is divided into two segments: The Northern and The Southern Heavens. In concentric circles, The Northern Heavens reach out from the Pole Star beyond the Milky Way to what reads as Capricanus, Scutum, Serpens, Libra, Sextans, Hydra, Monoceros, and Eridanus, while the replicate Southern Heavens at the bottom of the page helix out from Octars to the outer rims marked Canis Minor, Taurus, Pisces, Pegasus, Aquila and Delphinus.

If only it were that simple.

The last page divides New Zealand into North Island and South Island – just like Gearraidh – with five other major island archipelagos boxed neatly around them: the Samoan Islands, the Hawaiian Islands, the Society Islands, the Fiji Islands and – marvellously – the New Hebrides and New Caledonia, including the Loyalty Islands. What innocent, hopeful reading it all makes. There is a Bay of Plenty and Bream Bay and you need to look really closely to read the small brackets at the bottom of each boxed archipelago: Samoan Islands (to Gt Britain & U.S.A); Hawaiian Islands (to U.S.A.); Society Islands (to France);

Fiji Is (to Gt Britain); New Hebrides (to Gt Britain & France); New Caledonia (to France). A further, smaller box in the corner charts the whole lot as The Antipodes.

What is particularly interesting about the Atlas, however, are the early pages which set out the cosmological framework for the later cartography. Following rapidly on from the first page marked Astronomical Charts, you have – successively – Map Projections, World Physical, Arctic Regions, Antarctic Regions, World Geology, World Seismology, World Temperature, World Isobars and Winds, World Rainfall, World Climate, World Vegetation and Ocean Currents, World Population and World Political Divisions, with countless sub-sections within these general page headings, ranging from information titled Co-Tidal Lines and Ocean Drainage Areas to the Chart of Magnetic Variation, 1942.

Since these worlds were created, of course, we've had Hiroshima, Vietnam, the destruction of the Amazonian rainforest, Chernobyl, global warming and environmental pollution, all of which (and so much more) have minutely affected the way in which the tides move between the two parts of Gearraidh and how the people live and die.

The southern part of Gearraidh, perhaps because it lies a fraction closer to the east, perhaps because it benefits a fraction more from the Gulf Stream, perhaps because its people have been fractionally more diligent through the centuries in the use of drainage, or perhaps just out of sheer good luck and fortune, has suffered fractionally less from the enormous storm damage which has almost destroyed the more northerly section in recent years.

Just as, for instance, Tanganyika doesn't officially exist any more – or Persia, or French Indo China, or Manchuria – so the World Vegetation and Ocean Currents (pages 16 and 17 of Bartholomew's Atlas) have randomly altered. Those pink swirls on the map, which seemed so sure and definite: the North Atlantic Drift and the Gulf Stream and the West Wind Drift and the Canaries Current and the North Equatorial Current and the Equatorial Counter Current and so forth, have now become fluid, temperamental, variable, and ever-more dangerous. Of course, they were always thus so: only the fiction of cartography makes them then seem fixed, firm, sure, predictable and beautifully pink on the map.

If truth be told, they have always damaged Gearraidh – the two parts of it – in exactly the same way in which they damaged other parts of the world. It's just that in more recent times the damage feels greater, more haphazard, and more unfair.

The crux of the matter may be that the global change which has destroyed one part of Gearraidh more than another is the lesser issue. What, after all is Tanganyika now called? And in the exam paper, how do you answer this question: where was French Indo China, and what did the millions die there for?

Neighbours – sometimes immediate members of the same family – have watched helpless through binoculars as the violent storm has raged through the divided half of the island. They have watched friends, colleagues, sometimes sons and daughters, huddling by the rocks as the storm rages and the roofs fly, unable to do anything about it because the high tide has separated them, and it would be death to even venture out across the flooded strand.

Those tiny differences which have made the northerners northerners and the southerners southerners creep over the horizon, like lemmings, or midges, explaining away the global destruction by a mistake here or an error there, justifying the inequity – though not the iniquity – by this move or that, by this perception perceived or the other, by the small deeds done hundreds of years, perhaps only days, ago.

The chaos theory kicks in: and the belief that the fluttering of the butterfly's wings in Vietnam has awesome consequences in Wales, let us say. Who stayed out during the '45? On which side of The Great Disruption did the matter fall?

But it is all folly, as the storm gathers and sweeps all things before it. The blame lies elsewhere, beyond the binoculars, outwith the atlas. It is all arbitrary, fortuitous, capricious. Thank God. Thank God, you breathe. Not this time. This time it has passed us by. Again. The death belongs elsewhere, across the ford, across the strand, the other side of the tidal wave.

When the morning comes, the wreckage is everywhere: the sheds that belonged to southern Gearraidh lie broken in the open fields of the northern sector; the trees in the north have spun south, the grief and the anguish and the bereavement, as well as the relief, knows no compass.

Equally without reason, as if you randomly opened the Atlas at Spain and Portugal, by mid-day the sun shines through the watery clouds. The opaque light, which shows everywhere a different colour, floods the village, and the scattered wreckage and the surviving fields where the cattle huddle steaming by the slope. You suddenly realize that the tide has receded and that the white strand is shining, like a silver causeway, or a rosary, or a highway, or like the Milky Way.

The metaphors are endless and cause you to jump for joy, and as you glance up you reason that running across the stars which eternally link the Northern Heavens to the Southern Heavens are loads of young children, in both directions, holding hands, and skipping and jumping and whooping and laughing in their cartographic unity and perfection.

12

Carmina

The last resident of Carmina is Flora MacIntosh, who can't stop singing.

Whether singing requires or needs a listener is debatable: like writing, it is a solitary activity, though like making love ultimately pointless and distressing on its own.

So the song itself contains the audience. As she sings, alone on the vast empty island, she sings first of all to herself: not to herself as she is, old and grey and full of sleep, but to herself as she never really was, because that self was always just-about-to-be and is here now though still just-about-to be.

Her repertoire is vast and timeless, learned from those who learned it from those who learned it under the apple tree from the one who sang it before the fruit was hung. It is extensive and inclusive, bearing the blossoms of nursery-rhymes and laments, comedies and satires, loves and losses, wars and silences.

The songs tell with pride of the square of linen donned by a woman on the morning of her marriage; they tell with joy of the bare-backed horse-races on the Atlantic shoreline; they tell with distress of the time the clan chief fell in battle; they tell of how the only son was drowned within sight of the harbour.

Listening to the song is the young bride in the corner, the young man straddling the horse, the chief's eldest son as he sips the wine, the son's mother as she rocks backwards and forwards by the fire, old and grey and full of sleep.

The best definition I ever saw of all this was from Italo Calvino: 'the writer addresses a reader who knows more than he does; he invents a 'himself' who knows more than he does, to speak to someone who knows more still. There are no safe territories. The work itself is and has to be the battleground.'

Instinctively, Flora MacIntosh knows this. Each time the song is sung, it is for the first time, each word needs to be fresh-sprung or wrung from the soil, the victory has to be won each time because the young bride stands in the corner, because the cocky young man leans by the window, because the clan chief lies in the kist, because the grieving mother listens.

In Tolstoy's *War and Peace* Pierre walks through the battle because he understands this: he is safe because he is at the heart of the tempest; and each and every time I've listened to Flora's last song I am drawn to the heart of the storm: I become the bride, the horseman, the dead, the grieving.

All this costs, and what it has cost Flora MacIntosh is her right to die. She is condemned (if that is the right word) to live forever in order that she can bear witness, in order that she can sing, for and to the living and the dead; and not just those who've been, or are, but those queuing up on the next island waiting to be born, those whose songs have not yet been imagined.

The friends Flora had occupy the songs: for, you see, unlike all other islands where the residents are only catalogued at birth, marriage and death, the inhabitants of Carmina – for they were all singers – lie named in the university manuscripts, and croon on the celluloid tapes, and speak shamelessly of their communal poverty.

It shames me to name the few, but in remembering that there are no safe territories and that this itself is the battleground, it begins with Ann MacDonald, described as 'a crofter's daughter' of Bohunntin Bhile in Lochaber, who gave three songs, and finishes, without having even really begun, with singer number 216, John Stewart, described as 'a merchant' of Bachuill on the Island of Lismore.

They, of course, were only the coracles for the songs: the songs themselves were the sea on which the coracles sailed, brittle and infinitesmal and made out of broken bark. Like Ronan in his wild quest, the waves sheltered rather than threatened, comforted rather than terrified. It was not ignorance of the awesome power of the sea which enabled the South Uist woman to say, when she was emigrating and was asked what she would do when the great Atlantic storms came, *Nach bidh sinn am fàsgadh nan èiseanach, a' ghràidh?* – 'Shall we not be in the shelter of the big waves, my dear?'

And these big waves whip against the shore of Carmina, as Flora MacIntosh, aged 138, sits by the window, carding, and singing her songs. The more they beat, the more she sings, and not louder against the noise but softer against the silence.

It could so easily – so very easily – be a lament in the desert. Instead, it is (to use Carmichael's words) an invocation, an incantation, a supplication, a shielding, a charm, an augury, a cry against the noise. It is something functional, prosaic and necessary and because of that it is glorious, artistic and liberating. Like the cry of the gulls outside, which merely indicates that there are gulls outside, or like the shafts of the moon outside which merely indicates that the night is upon us, if you wish to reduce cosmology to information, living to life.

You could wish that this island were populated so that someone – anyone – could hear her song. You could despair, knowing that at this very moment they are (once again) bombing Basra and Baghdad. You could tear your hair out in anger that no one cares or listens. That no one appreciates or understands.

But as you move, without pausing, what you finally understand is this: her song depends on none of that. It is beyond both anger and despair, further on than the temporary and the partial. It plays where human response is most essential, in that vast hollow between the waves which can – of course – either shelter or drown.

13

Cumhnaigh

This is the lamentable island where the ghosts of the great persecuted, those who suffered injustice and those who joined the grand diaspora walk in endless defence of themselves.

The voices neither whine nor plead, but explain and justify, sometimes with hands outstretched, sometimes with hands clasped, persistent, reasonable, as if by the end of time it will become crystal clear that what happened to them was uncalled for, unasked for and unjustified.

Elsewhere, there is little doubt that the cavalcade continues. It is unthinkable to believe that at Auschwitz or in Siberia, for example, the congregation of the dead do not keep up the endless walk. 'For every casualty', as Cesare Pavese put it, 'resembles the survivor and demands to know the reason for his death from those who survive'.

But they walk here not because they demand to know the reason for their death – they know it full well – but to explain again and again the processes and the procedures and the practices which led to their death. Those arbitrary but essentially class-based circumstances which led them to being burnt out of their homes, or cleared from their land, or whipped into emigrant ships, or dying in the Ontario snow.

'They came for us at that time when it was neither quite night nor quite morning, but the in-between time, and I with a babe at the breast and seven children around me. My husband was away at the wars at the time, and I never saw him again, for they moved us from the land and put us on a ship and even if he survived the wars he wouldn't have known where to find us if he came back. I keep looking for him here, but have not yet found him.

'We had paid our rent but it made no difference, we didn't have the certificate to prove it, so we were evicted and moved away. It was winter and I was separated from my children: they were tall with red hair and the oldest – a girl – has a slight limp from the time she fell on the shore. You haven't seen them in your travels, have you?

'It was because of the fat hen. You see, we didn't have one and when the man came to collect the hen he got so angry he put us out of the house. If only I could find a fat hen, surely there must be a fat hen, maybe one of the small chicks has survived, but then again maybe the fox or the ferret ...'

And in this court of law, the evidence is all on one side and is absolute and overwhelming. Truth is the chief witness and no one responds to him, listening in silence to his inexorable claims that are undefended and unanswerable.

I ask the wandering women who make up the vast majority where the men are and they all say 'At the wars' or 'At the fishing', as if I'd asked where the moon was and they said 'in the sky'. And I ask where the other side are – those who caused this injustice, those who cleared them out of their homes for the sake of a fat hen. And they look at me with incomprehension, as if I'd asked in broad daylight where the moon was.

The moon is on the far side, shining on the dark side of the world which we cannot see from here. Wherever you are in daylight, the moon is elsewhere, eternally antipodean.

It has no light of its own, depending – like the earth itself – upon the flames of the sun for its reflected existence. So the moonlight that sweetly bathes the lovers in Australia is the sun which burns at 15,600,000 degrees Centigrade – more Hiroshimas than you can imagine stirring so many sweet dreams in the revolving night.

It takes great courage to be here, you realize: those who walk need to follow their instincts in their search for the lost husband, the lost child, the lost hen. When they come to a crossroads you notice that they invariably choose the one they have not travelled most recently, just in case this time, on that road, they come across the fair-haired one, or the limping one, or the small fat one. They have constant hope, eternal faith, against all the odds, despite the overwhelming evidence.

You think of culprits and causes as you watch them and you know this for sure – that even if all the perpetrators (actual and imagined) were roped together and led bare-foot and bare-arsed through the island, it would be like flinging a pail full of water at the sun: their guilt and shame would not suffice for the search for the fat hen. Their confession, or confessions, cannot atone for the losses suffered, for the deeds done which continue to be done, in their absence, daily.

And if they were to meet, you ask yourself – face to face, as it were? At random, you select the names, from Ghenghis Khan to Hitler, from Patrick Sellar to Colonel John Gordon of Cluny, and you know how wretched it would be, how they would excuse and justify themselves with their plausible petty arguments. How there was no choice, and how it needed to be done, and how it was for the people's (or the nation's or the world's) good that the Jews, or the disabled, or those who couldn't, at that moment, find the fat hen, were sent away. And you know how they would stand there frothing out of the corners of their mouths, or dribbling out of the sides of their pants, like madmen, while those they had punished would look at them with incomprehension, or fear or pity.

For what would you have them do? Deep inside, the part demand is for great revenge. But how to accomplish it? What value death when it is not long and lingering and conscious, for even torture has an end unless you take the ultimate leap and believe in the hell-fire which is unceasing and eternal? And you wish to be beyond mistakes, beyond errors of judgment: after all, there are degrees of wrong and guilt as well as stratospheres. Sometimes, you remember, the sun and the moon shine in the same sky, one fading and one rising, and what about when you rise high, on a rocket to outer space and see the firmament – earth, sun, moon and stars – hanging like toys above an infant's cot?

It is all perspective, and you choose: you choose the switch as the best you can do. So you alter their positions on the island, and those who committed the crimes (there! at last you've used the word) become the eternal victims of that very crime.

So the *maor-chearc* (the hen-bailiff) ... but was it really him? ... was he not just merely an underling and were the orders not really given by the *àrd-mhaor* (the head bailiff) or by the *bàillidh* (the factor) or – actually – the *ceann-cinnidh* (the clan chief himself), or at least his banker? ... is eternally consigned to searching for the fat lost hen. In a line of increasing guilt they walk endlessly in search of the unfindable.

No ferry leaves this island, which has no airport, and for a moment you are unsure of how to leave it, or whether you can ever leave it. Then you realize that issue is irrelevant, for the fords are passable and you can walk across them any time you want, day or night. The courage of the suffering holds you, but it is not your courage, which is of a differing variety. It is the courage to move on, even when all memory pleads with you to stay where you are, or have been.

14

Sileagh

It rains everywhere, but nowhere does it rain as often and as constantly and as heavily as in Sileagh – the hybrid Gaelic-Norse name, after all, means Rain Island!

From birth to death the inhabitants are covered in rain and the porches of their houses are brim-full of brollies and wellies and oilskins. The only shops on the island are the ones that sell raincoats and waterproofs, and the only industry is the water industry in all its shapes and forms, from the gathering and bottling and selling of water to the manufacture and making of all water-based machinery, ranging from hose-pipes to irrigation-hydrants.

The central myth is that when God made the heavens and the earth he looked down and instantly realized his mistake and wept, and that all these tears have since overflowed, as a blessing, upon Sileagh.

The complex water rituals which have always surrounded life on the island reflect that blessed myth: hardly any action, from pulling the new-born out of the womb to burying the old at sea, is done without due deference to water. The midwives bathe in *Tobar Mhuire* (Mary's well) before assisting in childbirth, the infants themselves are baptized in water the instant they are born, a river has been diverted to pass by the school gates so that the children, each morning as they enter school and every afternoon when they depart, can take off their shoes and dip their feet in the water before entering and leaving.

When these children become teenagers they are each set loose in an open canoe on the evening preceding their thirteenth birthday, and each of them, during the night, paddles round the island in a kind of solitary initiation ceremony. When couples marry, instead of being showered with confetti, they are sprayed with hoses of water and when people die, they are each carried for three days and three nights out to sea where they are buried at the setting of the sun.

The irrigation techniques developed over a long period of time on the island are worth special mention: a system is now in place which links every drop which falls with every other drop so that nothing is wasted. What falls from the skies is gathered from rivers and streams and tributaries and wells and dams and tanks and barrels. All of which is then fed into a central reservoir where (because of environmental damage) it is cleansed and purified before being piped back into the places from which it was first gathered – the rivers and streams and tributaries and wells and dams and tanks and barrels – before being re-distributed throughout the island in a complex network of pipes and hoses and channels and conduits and tubes and ducts to the various end-users, as they are now called: the people's homes, of course, and the school and the hospital and the shops and the various water industries.

What is revolutionary, however, is not the harnessing and distribution network, which is common enough every-where, but the fact that all of it is visible and celebratory rather than hidden and merely functional. Nothing is done invisibly and underground – all the pipes and hoses and tubes and ducts and so on and so forth are transparent and flagrantly run above ground, rather than being hidden, concealed, buried.

A network of colours distinguishes the varying functions and directions of these individual waters. The drinking water runs eastwards through translucent silver pipes, the water designed for bottling westwards through clear blue pipes, the water for industrial usage north through limpid green pipes and the water which will end up on the lawns and in the village fountains southwards through trans-parent yellow pipes.

But that, too, is the least of it: the boldest move of all was to construct a system which gives the same honour and dignity to the island's waste, which is not hidden away behind green netting or barbed wire fencing as elsewhere, but is publicly displayed with the same pride and conviction given to the sacred spring waters and the teeming rivers and overflowing lochs. So the urine and the faeces flow freely through their own lucid violet pipes without shame or camouflage.

As a direct consequence, tourism is one of the main by-industries of Sileagh: day visits and package tours to view these strange water works are readily available. Perhaps naturally enough, a good proportion of these rain-tourists are initially drawn to Sileagh (mostly now through the web at www.sileagh.co.uk) for the largely taboo or scatological reason that they will be publicly permitted to view the secreted. But once they spend the morning watching turds of all shapes and sizes and colours and contents floating by, it is remarkable how that initial morbid fascination wanes and gives way to genuine delight at the real marvels and wonders before their swimming eyes – the marvel of water moving, the wonder of the heavens harnessed to such effect and power and purpose.

They stand there in their raincoats and their wellington boots, sheltering under their multi-coloured umbrellas, staring at the rainwater pouring through the illuminated pipes, watching the streams turn into tea, the rivers into coffee, the waterfalls into coke, the lochs into soup, the clouds into those drips which keep the dying alive in all the wards of the world, and the heavens themselves (as well as the gathered earth beneath) into a single drop of water which is gathered at the end of the system. Down by the ocean's edge, there to drop intermittently, drop by drop, back into the ocean from which it came to feed the island upon which the drops drop, daily and without ceasing, drop by dripping drop.

15

Talamh

Most islands have created men to speak for them, though the rare one has produced women, and some even children, to tell the strange tale.

But Talamh is different because it is the land itself that tells the story, for those who now live on the island are not fluent in the old ways and have a different tale to tell in a language which the earth has not yet quite learned or grasped. That new tale is awesome and blinds the earth and brings it to silence because it is so new and static and different and strange.

If the earth were a young boy, this would be its first day at school, but if the earth were an aged woman would not all catechists gather round her to weep and repent? Instead, there are no similes or metaphors, just the visible face of things, the decay and the growth, the cities spreading like middle-age, the countryside moving from haystacks to leisure.

All earth has become property, and the island of Talamh is no exception – where once horses ploughed has become an internet cafe, where the cattle grazed is a construction site, where the *cas-chrom* (the peat-spade) dug deep is a leisure-centre, and the reputed site of the ancient sacred well lies groaning under the new road which connects village to village in the same way in which television luminously trades life across nations.

It would be easy, and wrong, to contrast the one with the other, when they really are the same thing, caught in different time-zones. The cheap way to go is to say the old was like this, while the new is like that, as if they were moral rivals feasting over good and evil. Surely they both ate (and eat) of the whole banquet. But that is not to say that they didn't have their individual voices, their own language, their own way of feeling things. It is not to say that they didn't have speech (or don't have speech), just like the Romans or the Chaldeans once had speech and just as the very young and the very old today have speech.

It is equally easy to say that language is as much a chasm as a bridge (and vice-versa), and either incomprehensible or perfectly clear, as if words or language – like islands – were symmetrical, definable, cartographic instead of being asymmetrical, irregular, imaginary. But like sentences, these islands are bumpy and jagged, indented by streams and fjords, hollowed by holes and quarries, raised by hills and mountains so that every step is a surprise. Once you climb a hill, you never know whether a loch or another hill lies on the far side, once you reach the far side of the wood you have no notion whether an impassable river or a trickling stream awaits you, once you arrive at a village you have no idea whether the dead or the living will be the ones who will speak to you.

So you try and impose your own pattern, your own language, until you realize it leads to deafness. You are always the stranger on the far side of language, obliged to listen – rather than to speak – even though the words may be new and harsh and brutal rather than old and sweet and re-assuring. For each has its voice and demands to be heard, the one in the silence and the other in the clamour.

Just as in love-making, there may be techniques to learn. It may be best to roll in the mud, or lie flat on your back or on your face without moving, or do so while gently rocking backwards and forwards in slow rhythm with what you imagine to be the in-built seismic movements of the earth itself. As in the old Indian movies, the most essential thing may to put your ear right next to the ground, though a tree, or a rock, or a shell from the shore will do just as well in some traditions.

The echo is called *mac-talla-nan-creag* which, literally translated, means the-son-of-the-hallway-of-the-rock because it was believed that the Echo lived in the grand entrance of the rocks where he shouted back whatever you called out to him as a warning to his master that a stranger was in the vicinity. There is always, in other words, an inter-mediary or a defender of the faith between yourself and the truth, between your shout and the silence, between your ear and the ground, between the earth and the sky.

In this new world, those echoes rebound, and you will need to be dead before you can began to appreciate what they had to say. It is always like that – just as you begin to understand your children, they are too far away; just as you really began to appreciate your mortality, the prefix knocks at the door demanding entrance.

But now, here, here on this island, lying in the cupped contour where your mother once played as a child, you believe you can hear. What you hear at first are the usual sounds, those whirling noises of wind and sand and sea and sky all clashing. The sand makes a kind of soft swishing sound, like the sound the warm potatoes used to make in her apron. The sea is the certain knowledge of her final illness, that distant thumping surge that removed her whole memory and made her paddle her feet in a bucket all day as if it was the wide ocean. The sky, all blue and azure with wispy speckled clouds, makes the noise of silence – a silence that is so absolute that it drowns out the high jet spuming somewhere west. That leaves the wind, which gusts and pauses, and rises and falls as if it too is unsure of its language, uncertain yet whether to bless or curse.

When you finally close your eyes in that place, you then hear the groaning of the very earth itself, of which you've become an integral part. You can hear the peat-bogs weep – listen! The former corn field which once covered the football pitch and the small housing estate whispers in the wind – cut me down, I'm all ripe and golden and yellow! And you hear, somewhere far off, the clanking of chains and the neighing of the harnessed horses trying to free themselves from the slides and the chutes and the climbing frames now covering the wild paddock they once had for themselves.

Hay-stacks and corn-ricks once stood where the picnic-tables and chairs now stand, and in the evening light you can hear the slow champing of the brown cows as they wend their way in between the cars and the motor-homes parked on the terraces where the cattle-fields used to stretch.

You imagine you hear a bull bellowing in the distance from the direction of the stone hut he used to inhabit and which you were so frightened of passing when you were young, but that archaic memory only turns out to be the passing of a car's stereo as it travels northwards through the island, with a young man's elbow leaning out the window and the girl beside him smiling, without any fear.

16

Cànaigh

On some islands you feel constrained and your vocabulary diminishes, but on Cànaigh terminology is released, like a flock of wild birds in winter, and speech runs away with you. It is like being liberated after a long imprisonment when you want to kiss the grass of words, breathe in the air of syntax, run through the wind of language, like a child after school, like a lamb after fleecing, like an oration from the tomb.

You suddenly realize, on Cànaigh, that all things are permitted and that language no longer needs to be careful, considered, cautious. The people here are so in love with language that nothing hurts – not swear words, or misuse of language, or abuse of words, or slips of the tongue, or ungrammatical grammar, or hyperbole or simile or metaphor or newly-minted words beyond the furthest knowledge of any known, or unknown, lexicographer living or dead.

Different narratives excite people, and when you switch from the 1st person singular to the 3rd person objective, or from the active present to the subjunctive, no one bats an eyelid. On the contrary, they imagine that you are articulating a new form of expression, liberating the language from the conventions which have stultified it, and vigorously applying the elasticity and plasticity of language which they believe to be at the very heart of living.

As you walk along the village street in Canaigh and suddenly remember a word – let's say 'manatee' for instance – your natural instinct is to pause and make sure you know what it means (it's actually any large aquatic plant-eating mammal of the genus *Trichecus*, with paddle-like forelimbs, no hind limbs, and a powerful tail – derived from the Spanish *manati* and the Carib word *manattoui*) and that you know the context in which you might use it before you ever speak it out. But as soon as you remember you are on Cànaigh you of course shout out immediately, and at the top of your voice if you want, 'Manatee.' Before you know it a crowd will be round you asking you to say it again with the distinct variant pronunciations, and a vigorous debate is likely to ensue as to the many ways in which that singular could be used, in conversation, poetry, prose or theological intercourse.

Suddenly, as you sit in church, or in the middle of a concert, someone will remember the nomenclature of the elementary rules of Grammar and will cry out: 'Vowels! Consonants! Spelling and Aspiration! Pronouns Personal and Possessive!' From the other corner a voice joins in: 'The Verb! The Adjective! Pronouns! Nouns! Declensions of Nouns!' and then another in the far corner: 'The Second Declension!' and one next to him; 'The Third Declension!' and the one next to him: 'The Fourth Declension'. Next thing the entire congregation – or concert part if you will – are standing collectively calling out: 'Irregular Declension! Numerals Cardinals! Numerals Ordinals! Prepositions! Prepositional Pronouns!' before they all start dancing and swaying and singing in full charismatic-style: 'The Conjugation of Irregular Verbs! Defective Verbs and Defective Auxiliary Verbs! Idioms!' And of course there is always one rascal who cannot resist the final 'Amen!'

This evangelical liberality with language spills over into normal everyday usage, of course. In the middle of a conversation – let's say at the local food store – two women are standing in the queue.

'Beautiful morning.' says the first – let's call her Janice.

'Marvellous,' says the other – let's call her Jemima. 'I feel like a peach in the ocean.'

'Who knows then that tomorrow will not be an orchard?'

'She hung in time, like an apple defying gravity.' responds Janice.

'It was all memory, of course,' says Jemima. 'The meaning of being a leaf weeping over the ascending fruit.'

And a round of applause breaks out from the other shoppers, beautifully distracted for these few moments from the essential shelves of survival.

Naturally, it takes a while to get used to this freedom of speech, this autonomy of language and sovereignty of choice. Rapid case and declension and tense changes initially confuse you until you confess to yourself that all language is a switchback ride across the machair or the prairie or the mountain or the desert or the ocean or whichever plateau takes your fancy, in which you need planning, nerve, commitment, creativity and supplies to survive.

Let's take the machair, for instance, which is the most relevant landscape in the island context. The machair is that sandy portion of land which stretches between the shoreline and the village settlements. It is not only the most beautiful part, especially in those months between May and September when it is sequentially – and often enough simultaneously – carpeted in clover and pansies and sea pinks and the green and golden shoots of potatoes and corn and barley, but also the most fertile and productive.

The linguistic (or agricultural) needs you have on the machair all depend on what you're there for. Once upon a time you needed the vocabulary as well as all the tough technical skills of horsemanship, but in today's leisure world the machair has largely become a place of contemplation, much as our great Cathedrals have become coffee shops rather than centres of worship

Just as almost no-one does the Latin Mass any more, so just about nobody ploughs or works the machair any more: the Confiteor and the Introit Antiphon, just like the breech-chains and the bridle-rein, have been left to medievalists and retrospective television programme-makers, so the language connected with these activities has become, just like the old iron ploughs which litter the machair, rusty and corroded, forgotten and disused.

So when you walk the machair today you need to imagine

more than you need to act, and your language responds accordingly. You can, of course, be completely passive, watching the machair as you would watch television, like a distant phenomenon, a thing given, but the obligation is to interact with that environment. See how the lilies of the field grow – I declare to you that Solomon in all his glory was not clothed like one of these! See how purple – how mauve – the clover is! See the way in which these potatoes – are they Kerr's Pinks, after all? – are flourishing! See how this field has gone fallow where the barley used to grow, and don't you remember those Autumn days (and how we thought they would last forever, which of course they have) when these fields were covered in reapers, one with a scythe here, a woman gathering the ears of corn there, the children playing hide-and-seek in the hay-stooks over yonder? Then you would hear (one time) the distant neighing and then clink-clanking of the horses and the rattling of the green – why were they always green? – carts truttling down through the village road, which later on turned out to be the far-off sweet and heady smell of paraffin smelt before you actually heard the tractors – the Massey Fergusons were best – bumping their way along the rickety-rackety roads.

My God, you realize, you could turn it all into a story, a fiction, a film, a wondrous work of the imagination which would tell it – or show it – how it really was. Do you remember the Italian neo-realists you ask yourself? And that time you snogged in the back of the Cameo cinema while supposedly watching the great film *Ladri di Biciclette*

– Bicycle Thieves – ah, what a film! Now there you have it: real people doing miraculous things, or was it the other way round?

You get carried away, forgetting (what a word!) that there is someone listening, that there is an audience, a readership to whom you have some responsibility (ah – now there's a word!). The responsibility for what? To entertain, to educate, to amuse, to enlighten, to humour, to tolerate, to love? (ah now, that's the word!).

And to love! To love the reader, as the crofter loved his horse – functional and aesthetic – as the harvester loved the machair – functional and historical and aesthetic – as the dweller of Cànaigh loves his language both fictionally and functionally. And the responsibility within that love? To behave with due dignity and decorum? Not to grieve or hurt, not to puff up or diminish, but to speak the truth within that great hymn written by the small man with the crooked nose who punched out the big definitions – about it all being patient, kind, unenvious, unboastful, courteous, selfless, calm, forgiving, joyous, protective, trusting, hopeful, persevering. No wonder he finished with the flourish that love never fails.

Unlike us, as we drift now down towards the pier at Cànaigh collectively growing quieter, more silent, though some are having a last wild flurry and you can hear the great words liberated like the fairy leaves of the bog-cotton in the Autumn wind – catch them as they rise with a desperate shout into the air: 'plissè' and 'circadian' and 'edaphic' and 'gingko' and 'rhomboideus' and 'zuchhetto' and a thousand and one other words as luscious as summer sweets, as sensuous as the thought of her long bare thigh.

All too soon, we are back on the ferry and the pier-worker is dismantling the gangway and unleashing the ropes which release us back into captivity and we all stand on the deck leaning over the gang-rail for a last long lingering look as we round the bay. The island disappears out of sight as we all look at each other, now weighing up our words, but imagining that we heard the pier-worker shout out his farewell which, to me at least, sounded like *ioma-chruthachd* (multiformity) but on the other hand may just have been *seagh ma-thà*, which simply means 'Okay – that's it then.'

17

Mnathaigh

The fact that women reign on this island lends weight to the argument that the island's name is simply derived from the Gaelic name for women – *mnathan* – though others (and plenty women scholars among them) argue that the real derivation of the word is from the word *mathan*, without the *n*, which means 'bear' – hence Bear Island.

Jokes abound, of course, about the similarity between *mnathan* and *mathan* – women and bear – and secondary jokes about bearing and child-bearing and bear-baiting are common, but the reality still is that here – and here only – women have been given public as well as private status, authority as well as responsibilities, liberty in as well as the load of love.

It's not just, or merely, that women hold positions of public power and authority – that, on the surface at least, is common enough – but that the rights given to them – and aren't all rights given, not taken? – are theirs by virtue of an ordeal that only they have passed.

All societies, tribal or otherwise, ancient or contemporary, are based on ordeal: that of being born, being educated, being successful – whether in love or work or finance or health – being popular, being handsome, being useful, being articulate, being male, being female. Big Brother always ruled.

The rewards, of course, are uneven and never work out equitably: the most educated woman in the world, for example, can be the least successful; the most articulate writer in the universe can be the poorest; the most handsome man on the planet can be the unhappiest. Where, tell me, has fortune favoured the brave – have not time and circumstances struck down the best and the bravest, just when they were on the crest of Everest, just when the victory was within their grasp, right there at the top of their Mount Gilboa, just before the final text votes poured in?

But the ordeal on the island of Mnathaigh is not that of the warrior: no status is given to the one who can manage to haul the gold-encrusted sword out of the iron forge; no great esteem is given to the one who can run fastest while holding a barrel of herring on each shoulder; no great praise is given to the one with the fastest horse or the biggest pig-house or the best cock.

Instead, regard is given to those who pass the ordeals by virtue of abolishing them in the process, transforming them from rituals into sacraments, from trials of strength into ceremonies of innocence.

Take, for instance, the ordeal of gaining public office, in which communal favour is slickly courted: here in Mnathaigh, the one who gets the least votes is elected as a guarantee that she or he will have least favours to pay back. Or again, take the ordeal of gaining a university qualification: here in Mnathaigh the degree is given to you before you start, so that the shame of losing it at the end guarantees a 100% success rate.

The fact that, in general, women have emerged triumphant from this system has less to do with gender, of course, than with conditioning, in so far as one can distinguish between the two. The hunter-gatherer, the warrior and the testosterone-filled male have a long, arduous pedigree, as do the mothers and wives and daughters, and only a foolish legislator would deny them or pass them by.

So in Mnathaigh they don't: instead, these are all given the first bite of the cherry, the first crack of the whip, the first skirl o' the pipes – whichever clichè you least like. But on this one condition: that the consequences of that bite, that crack, that skirl are then judged, with finality, by those traditionally considered at the other end of the scale – the weak, the infirm, the feeble, the old, the demented, the barren, the divorced, the separated, the rejected, the abused. Not one piece of proposed legislation from the former has stood that sacramental test.

The consequence – and it has taken a time which cannot be measured by human standards – is that the island community of Mnathaigh is ruled by women but governed by the broken. The latter know whom they can trust, but the former also know that they cannot trust themselves: in that, they have passed the toughest test, and have consequentially transformed that final ordeal – the ordeal of power – into the sacrament of love.

18

Armaigh

The military own and run this island, as they must own and operate cities and nations and continents and galaxies elsewhere.

This is no *Rockets Galore*, with its humour and whimsy, but a hard, cold place where the dead are buried in steel and the living are sent on missions of glory in the certitude that they will soon join their encased comrades.

The island itself is well chosen: a jagged outcrop with a long strip of grass in the middle, so that the commandoes can climb to the jagged heavens by day and night and arrive or depart with the living or the dead at any time they choose. Fjords and cliffs and escarpments incise the western shore of the island, again making it an ideal playground for the grown-up games of death. Men in camouflage, knives held tight between their teeth, and faces blackened with soot, practice ascending silently to throttle the sleeping guards at the top.

But that kind of thing is archaic, and really only a pastime, or for the entertainment of the documentary crews who sporadically arrive to film the 'fascinating relationship' (as a recent TV promo put it) 'between fighters and fulmars', for the real activity of death on this island lies hidden, literally, beneath the surface.

For there, as the fulmars screech above and the TV crews quaff their beer in the local pub 'The Dove Inn', nuclear and chemical death is daily being organized on precision scale. As in something out of HG Wells – or is it Jules Verne? – complex and vast underground tunnels and bunkers have been constructed under Armaigh which reach out unto the very ends of the earth.

These tunnels and bunkers criss-cross the sub-sea globe, connecting all the land-masses and power-centres of the world in an intricate, though often contradictory, network. It is a physical as well as a metaphysical web: not merely the electronic world wide web, but an intricate system of physical passages which connect the death-merchants of London with those of Washington, those of Washington with those of Moscow, and those of Moscow with those of Beijing.

Now – as then – Armaigh remains the access-point to a remarkable and hellish universe. In military mythology the place remains a symbol almost of purity and innocence, and certainly of courage and valour – this isolated, lonely, rocky outcrop which through great sacrifice and daring and endeavour has ensured the triumph of the civilized world in these oh-so-savage and brutal times.

When you see the island of Armaigh, whether from the air or from the sea or on television or from postcards, you have no notion that this small rocky outpost is just the visible tip of an invisible labyrinth. Like all other islands in the archipelago, it hides far more than it reveals.

The language or discourse used to describe the traders of death is, of course, completely different from that which I've chosen to use here: in this vast underground world, language – like everything else – is submerged, coated, protected and disguised.

In this submerged world, merchants are called politicians, death is called 'non-operational', and all war – of course – is against terror.

The fascinating thing is that the sub-sea network is an exact mirror image (i.e. as in all mirrors, an inverted image) of the world above. In other words the distances, let's say between Moscow and Washington, are the same underground as above ground (or, for that matter, in the air). But – just as in a mirror – in this sub-sea world Moscow is where Washington would be, and vice-versa. What you have here is a world where everything replicates itself exactly and precisely, but through an inverted cartography.

The history of the development of the rocky outpost of Armaigh as the hub-centre of this transposed world is long and complicated, but easy enough to understand. It generally falls into the category of these many remote places (such as the South Pacific Islands) which over time have been militarily used to explode atomic bombs, test biological weapons, fire experimental rockets and store nuclear waste.

The slightly different thing about Armaigh is that the underground and sub-sea dimensions of this work began at an early stage – when the military first took over the island, immediately following the dispersal of the people, they did so largely because of the vast, underground network of fissures and chasms and caves and tunnels that the island was blessed with. The indigenous mythic history of the island ascribes these natural gorges and abysses to the goddess Sithuana who was said to have originally carved them out, using the bones of dead sailors, as hiding places for her children fleeing the wrath of the sea god Nurthuagh.

But the holes and cavities and ravines and canyons were heaven for the military visionaries of the time. Here, they thought (correctly), were the ideal natural infernos for carrying out their experiments and the initial underground heaven proved to be even more wonderful than they had ever hoped to imagine. For to their surprise and delight initial explorations revealed that the inferno was deeper and more substantial and far more widespread than they had anticipated. In short, their heaven – or hell – was universal and not just localized.

One man (who was later awarded the posthumous VC) was initially sent down, but like the hero who followed the piper into the Cave of Gold, he never returned, and on the rare windless nights in mid-Atlantic can still be heard by passing ships knocking on the vaults of the ocean, either for the way out or the way in.

But the loss of the initial hero only encouraged the military planners: if the best had disappeared, they argued, then it only proved that the tunnels and shafts beneath Armaigh were longer and more interesting than they thought. So – being military planners – they decided to double the operation each time, sending two, then four, then eight, then sixteen, then thirty-two, then sixty-four, then one hundred and twenty-eight, then two hundred and fifty-six, then five hundred and twelve, then one thousand and twenty-four, then two thousand and forty-eight, then four thousand and ninety-six, then eight thousand one hundred and ninety two, then sixteen thousand three hundred and eighty-four, then thirty two thousand seven hundred and eighty six, then sixty five thousand five hundred and thirty six soldiers down into the dark shafts, of whom not one returned.

But the magic door was opened when they reached the six figure sum. Once the next arithmetic batch – one hundred and thirty one thousand and seventy-two of them – were sent down into the caverns, the generals and the political merchants hit gold, as it were. Dante Ali Baba's cave sprung open. One came back alive speaking all the known languages of the world (initially – naturally – they thought he had been driven mad) and told of the marvels and the wonders he had seen in the sub-sea world: more than a hundred thousand corpses, right enough, heaped throughout the vast underground caverns but beyond that the paradise that they had been seeking. Here was the man who had, like Satan in the book of Job, returned from roaming through the earth and going to and fro in it.

He told of all he had seen from below: the Brandenburg Gate and the Forbidden City and the Golden Gate Bridge and the Victoria Falls and the ancient ruins of Machu Pichi, and he told it in all the indigenous languages of the world – how, when he had descended through the initial shafts and caverns and crawled past the infinite dead he had gradually realized that someone was crawling with him, sometimes alongside him, sometimes beneath him, sometimes upside-down above him. Knee for knee, palm for palm, a turn of the head for a turn of the head, like an inverted shadow, and it took him some time to realize that he was following himself and that the walls of the warrens were fractured mirrors made from the frozen substances of the earth's crust.

'So I followed myself' the man said, 'and he led me to all the treasures of the world, which ultimately all lead back here with the trail of blood which I've left behind', and he showed all the generals and merchants his wrists, which he had severed in two with a jagged piece of stalactite. 'And when I ran out of blood, halfway across the world, my shadow covered the other half for me, cutting his wrists so that we would not run short of blood before we got back here to show you the trail that leads to the ends of the earth.'

And he stood there, pale as death, with his ghost, pointing the way backwards.

So the generals and the merchants began following the trail of blood beneath the earth, and set up guard-posts and watch-stations and observation-towers and training-camps and unit-bases and rocket-ranges and military-establishments and research-centres and front-line camps and – eventually – military cities with their accompanying political wings all over the world under the sea and the earth.

As on the earth above, this subterranean world was divided between the superpowers, except that the cartographic balance of the earth was inverted, with the eastern part of the sub-sea world given to the west and the western part given to the east. 'That way' said one wise general 'we'll make absolutely sure no hostilities ever break out, for if they do, up there the east will destroy the west and the west will destroy the east, whereas down here the east will destroy the east and the west the west. Now that is Mutually Assured Destruction and a sure-fire way to guarantee everlasting peace!'

They held a party too in these early days, for the wisdom and courage and sheer doggedness which had made it possible for the civilized world – as opposed to the terrorists – to gain control of the entire subterranean universe.

'Imagine', said the leading merchant, 'if we hadn't been prepared to sacrifice these first one hundred thousand soldiers. Imagine if they – the terrorists – had gotten down here before us. What a threat and danger that would be to all the worlds.'

So to celebrate, they ascended the cliff-edges and snared all the fulmars and gannets and puffins that remained. The feathers they made into pillows. Their oil into fuel.

And then they drank a sweet rich wine redder than the blood of sacrificed multitudes.

19

Cumanta

Just in case you begin to think that all the islands in the archipelago are full of extra-ordinary events and people and histories, let me introduce you to the Island of Cumanta, which basically means ordinary or commonplace – thus the Island of the Commonplace or, if you prefer, Ordinary Island.

Here is where nothing extraordinary ever happens: an island chock-full of ordinary people, some happy, some sad, some old, some young, some male, some female, some drunk, some sober, some employed, some unemployed. It has all the things that other ordinary islands have, though none of the things that other ordinary islands have. It contains no mosques or synagogues or kingdom halls and the temples are all ancient and sacred and in ruins.

It has a Post Office, however, and five different kinds of church to meet the needs of the ordinary worshippers: Roman Catholic, Church of Scotland, Free Church, Free Presbyterian Church and Baptist, though a recent born-again charismatic denomination calling itself The Church of God – presumably meaning that all the other five churches are not quite the church of God – has also just begin to satisfy the needs of the ordinary born-again worshipper.

121

This ordinary island has five hotels, ten pubs, two piers, one airport, a library, a go-karting centre, a community hall, an aquadome, five wind-farms, three quarries, a local newspaper, eight potteries and four craft centres, one of them an internet cafè, and a Co-op.

Nothing extraordinary either has happened in the history of Cumanta. Of course there have been the usual wars and famines and pestilences, and the time the winter flood swept the local school and all its 100 children – and the five teachers – to their deaths, but the ordinary people of Cumanta know very well that these tragedies are commonplace and have been visited, at one time or the other, upon the whole world.

Cumanta has produced no extraordinary warriors – if you except Dòmhnall Mòr a' Chlaidheamh Bhig, who was Napoleon's right-hand man throughout the winter campaign – and no extraordinary explorers – if you exclude Ruairidh Dhòmhnaill Thormoid Bhig, who was the first person to round Cape Horn while strapped to the mast – and no extraordinary poets – if you exclude the bardess Sìleas nighean Alasdair, whose epic verse was once compared with Homer by the late great Sorley MacLean who, of course, was an extraordinary bard but had no connection with Cumanta.

The mythology of Cumanta is also ordinary, in that it traces its physical origins to God himself, creating Cumanta out of the common soil and the people of Cumanta out of the common dust, except for the women, who were created out of an ordinary rib. Let us be clear however, that although the rib was ordinary, the hand of the Maker was extraordinary: ordinary things with an extraordinary God might just about sum up the ordinary Cumanta theology.

Each day on Cumanta the ordinary people go about their ordinary chores in ordinary ways: the ferryman, for instance, wakes beside his ordinary (though somewhat overweight) wife in an ordinary (king-size) bed, does an ordinary yawn – though his wife complains that he opens his mouth too wide and that it looks like the pictures of the Grand Canyon she's seen on television – then puts his feet on the ordinary carpet (bought in the prime of his manhood in Cairo when he was a sea-going sailor) and from there walks to the toilet to do an ordinary pee before having an ordinary breakfast of ham and eggs and black pudding and two fried eggs and a couple of sausages, then going on his ordinary motor-bicycle – a converted Yamaha 1000cc which was once owned and raced by the legendary Paulo Rossi – down to the pier where he operates the ferry backwards and forwards all day carrying ordinary people of all tribes and languages between the island and the mainland.

Any one of the 3000 residents could be described in that ordinary fashion – the nurse and doctor, the mechanic and joiner, the mother and child, the electrician and plumber. An ordinary drunk sits slumped at the end of the bar staring into his whisky, vaguely trying to remember that time he played shinty for Scotland at Croke Park in Dublin, and how he scored the winning goal. An ordinary father and husband is lying in the local hospital staring at the tube which is keeping him alive. An ordinary girl is down by the edge of the woods, refusing for the umpteenth time to go in there with her boyfriend who is now calling her 'chicken'.

The difficulty is to know where the lie originated – when did the most extraordinary thing that ever happened become ordinary? When did he or she who was made or emerged out of dust or rib or plasma begin to think or believe that the miraculous – whichever way you look at it – was ordinary and commonplace? Who first shrugged his shoulders when the blazing sun rose (once again) out of the morning sky? Ah, John Donne! Who was the first to be indifferent to his lover's hot kisses, his mother's birth-pains, his enemy's death? Who gave Cumanta its name, and defined its history and mythology and has given this people this definition of themselves and their place as ordinary and common, making them citizens of a falsehood?

What in fact does ordinary mean? The *Concise Oxford Dictionary* (the one to hand) describes it thus: 'regular, normal, customary, usual; boring, commonplace'. And common? Defined as this: 'occurring often, ordinary, without special rank or position, shared, low-class, vulgar, inferior, of the most familiar type, of lesser importance'

Each of these dictionary words, like all of our definitions, are essentially political: there is hardly a single word any of us uses which doesn't carry with it a whole world of meanings. Every adverb drags a library behind it, every noun a civilization, every adjective a universe, every declension a time. When I see the sun set I think of my father. The round moon reminds me of Dòmhnall Iain Dhunnchaidh the bard. Every time I smell chestnuts I think of the girl with the brown eyes I saw as I climbed out of the Paris metro.

She was milking the cow on Cumanta the last time I saw her, just the other day. It was late in the evening and the black cattle had come down from the high hills for their evening milking. You could hear them lowing all the way down, like the siren of ships in the fog, with the dogs yapping in the distant farmyard. It was one of those evenings you often get in Cumanta – an ordinary evening, you might say – with the sky turning pink just before the sun takes its bath, and that was when I saw her, climbing out of the red tractor which had just trundled down from the turnip fields where she'd been working all afternoon.

She was wearing red overalls and her auburn hair was – as in one of those romantic films – billowing in the breeze. She smiled across the fields and I could see her brown eyes glittering with all the sex with which they glittered that other hot day in Paris. She was radiant, like the setting sun itself, and I watched her as she sat down on the milking stool beside the first large cow and sensuously squeezed the distended teat, releasing the milk into the tin pail.

And as she milked she sang, like an act of heroism, one of those ancient songs which make you believe that life has – just at that very moment – been invented. One of those ordinary songs which the people of Cumanta have in their thousands for such a time and such a moment as this.

20

Turaseo

The Island of Turaseo is where all your regrets are made well. Here is where you get the second – or the tenth or hundredth – chance to right the wrong, or at least to make (or re-make) the choice you wished you'd made all along, but didn't, through fear or lack of courage, through blindness or foolishness, through mere forgetfulness.

Such as that time you were dying to ask her out – remember her now with all the imaginative accuracy you can muster! – but didn't, because you were afraid that when you went up to her to say 'Will you come out with me tonight?' she would laugh at you and say 'You?! Do you think I would go anywhere near a worm like you?' But this time, here on the special island of Turaseo it is all different. She melts into your arms and you kiss, and that kiss lasts forever and she is eternally young like she was that moment you first set eyes on her, her hair tumbling over her shoulders and that wicked way she smiled and the way her small breasts were set to rip her school blouse apart and the way her knees drew you like the ocean every time she sat in the class and her mini-skirt acted like a tide, rising and receding.

Much as people still go on pilgrimage to Iona, folk come here to Turaseo from the very ends of the earth. They come, old and young, rich and poor, black and white, male and female, from every tribe and nation, and speaking every language under the sun, to get that second shot at the thing. You would think regret belonged to the old or those who visibly carry the burdens of failure, but Turaseo dispels all these false preconceptions: remorse haunts the young, disappointment burdens the rich and famous.

Although no map is given to anyone who arrives on Turaseo, the burdened instinctively find their ways to those places which specialize in their particular sorrow. Perhaps it's as simple as the fundamental law of physics, or just that like draws like, but the failed lovers gather in the hollows of the hills, the unachieved workers spread themselves on the sandy shorelines, and those whose regret is nameless congregate in the green meadows down by the wells where the atonement is fluid and watery.

But don't be mistaken – Turaseo is not some kind of vague mystical experience. It is neither a transcendental nor a sacred place. No religious services of any kind take place here. No-one (at least visibly) prays. No-one lays hands on anyone else, no-one meditates or gets in touch with their inner selves, no-one is healed by a magic well or by consecrated water or by crystal stones.

The fact is (probably) that everyone who arrives is already healed, for the reputation of Turaseo has gone before it. No-one comes here without knowing why they've come – it's not a tourist destination, though it invariably draws tourists who, of course, leave worse than they arrived. No passing ships or ferries or planes call at Turaseo

just for the hell of it: a powerful myth is also abroad that to
set eyes or foot on Turaseo without a need for expiation is
to call down a curse upon yourself and all those you love.

So those who come to Turaseo have all already made the
decision that matters. They have already recalled and
memorized and lived and re-lived that missed opportunity.
The moment they said No when they ought to have said
Yes; the time they said Yes when they ought to have said No;
that time he refused her hand, or she refused his apology;
that time he turned away, or she put her face to the wall; that
time he chose the wrong word, she chose the wrong
moment, the wrong person, the wrong partner, the wrong
city, the wrong job, the wrong island.

So they arrive here – failed poets and novelists and
archeologists and bank-managers and fishermen and
priests and ministers and rock-stars – to affirm that where
they are is fine, simply because they could be no place – or
indeed no-one – else. On that journey to Turaseo they have
already weighed all the possibilities and probabilities: the
possibility that, after all, she would have turned away and
rejected him; the probability that even had they moved to
Australia that time, things still would not have worked out.

Across the oceans they come, balancing the likelihoods,
counter-balancing the desires. Her eternally young image
competes with what he has become; her moment of
rashness years ago evaluates itself against the person she
has become just because of that moment of foolishness.
Weights and counter-weights compete, and of course on
the journey, alone, the best of both worlds is lived. The

impossible is fulfilled, time wheels backwards and the now that is now and the then that was then become the now that was then and the then that is now, and the choice made becomes impeccable, forgiven, and eternally right.

Some carry things with them on the boat journey – mirrors and brushes and pencils and lap-tops and cameras – and make other things out of them as they travel, but most take nothing but themselves and make something else out of that as well. But this is the point of the story: no-one actually ever sets foot on Turaseo. For as soon as the boat arrives at the pier it immediately departs without putting the gangway down and all those who've travelled wave a fond farewell to the familiar hollows in the hills and to the familiar sandy shorelines and to the familiar green meadows down by the wells where the atonement is fluid and watery.

They have all been there, time and again, without ever setting foot on the island, and as soon as the ship arrives back in home harbour it embarks again, fully crewed and loaded, departing one more time.

21

Cuartaigh

Had we chosen a different mode of travel – say by canoe or by foot or even by air – we would have viewed and visited different islands, which were not on the route we took, and even the islands we visited would have approached us differently as we rowed, or swam, or flew towards them, or above them, or by them.

From a kayak, for instance, we would have been dwarves and from planes, giants. Instead, the archipelago has been like writing a sentence or climbing a rock-face or walking a rope across the chasms: something you take word by word or toe-hold by toe-hold or step by step. You dare not pause for breath in case the words collapse; you dare not look up for fear of becoming paralyzed; you dare not look down in case of vertigo.

Suddenly you're there, miraculously, at the far side of the sentence, which now looks so given, or on the top of the mountain-face which now looks so jagged, or – like Blondin – on the other side of the chasm, which now looks so empty and so very far away.

And as you pause, on the far side of the sentence, or on top of the mountain, or on the other side of the gorge, what you think of are the countless number of alternative sentences you could have written and didn't, and the innumerable beautiful rock-climbs which still lie in wait in the Alps and the Pyrenees. These gorges and canyons which you could now try and cross, not just on a tightrope, but doing so while cycling, or while juggling or even while juggling and cycling, and carrying two scantily-clad women on your shoulders. The fun you could have if only you trusted your freedom.

So the alternative islands rise up, calling for attention, like forgotten ghosts in the moonlight, like the next page in Ivor's comic sneaking round the corner, like your father or mother or son or daughter or teacher or neighbour or friend or enemy or ancestor or descendant calling, drawing your attention to their needs, their aches and pains, their hopes and desires.

The island where everyone permanently sits down and the one where everyone always stands up. The island which is now just a plasma screen remotely viewed from your living room. The one which doesn't exist, because no one cared sufficiently. The heart-shaped island where everyone constantly falls in love; the coffin-shaped island where everyone hates. That one over there made out of pixels of my grandfather's faded photographs.

The ones we haven't yet discovered or invented. The ones taken by the tsunamis and the brand-new ones emerging out of the crumbling dust of the earth. The ones turning to parchment before our very eyes. The ones we haven't yet named or imagined, which might yet fit the words we haven't conceived of. The Eden where an original language remains capable of deciphering the continuing fiction.

Those which have irrevocably changed since we last called upon them, moments or days or centuries ago. Those chapters which have already altered since we read them, to which we could add words or subtract gravity. Take Colathaigh, for example, where a substantial counter-movement has now begun on the beautiful remote east coast.

According to rumour, groups of young men have taken to returning completely to the old ways and have become totally immersed in ancient practices and dogmas which, they forcefully argue – the news has poured all over the other islands – are eternally relevant and therefore as appropriate for the 21st as for the 11th century.

Apparently, this includes walking backwards blind-folded, a practice erroneously lifted from an ancient bardic scroll which had lain gathering dust for years in the local library. It is said that a zealous young man, named Airais, recently came across the relevant passage while studying the sacred poetry of the renowned mystic Raghnall Dall MacMhuirich.

In one particular section of Raghnall Dall's famous epic *Sìneadh nan Speuran* (The Expanse of the Heavens) the mystic discovers the true meridian of the heavens by first walking blindfolded backwards across the known earth: when the blindfold is released, the sudden light is so dazzling that he sees beyond known space, right into infinity itself.

Various Celtic scholars and a number of secular psychologists have since explained the medieval vision in terms of what they call 'darkened memory': that capacity of the mind to retain and imagine all things in the darkness, which are then either dissolved or magnified with sudden exposure to light.

It seems that Airais has taken the text absolutely literally and has gathered round him a whole host of young men who are currently walking blindfolded backwards, in the effort to reach ultimate illumination and revelation.

The woman who ran breathlessly northwards with the news has joined the rest of the islanders waiting fearfully for the inevitable clash between them and those others, led by Caleb, careering forward heedlessly, no matter the consequence.

It may all, of course, be rumour though several deaths have already been reported, some verified by video.

'Remember us' the dead cry from the seaside graves. 'And us!' shout the drowned of the seas. 'And don't forget me. And me. And me. And me,' call out the clouds and the big river where the coach-and-horses once sank and the blue mountain where the fairy folk lived, once upon a time. When they were born they were a thousand years old and only ever grew young.

Then there is the girl from no island, who came for a visit and stayed.

Born in the east end of the great city, she arrived at the end of the gap year and never departed. Not because the island is especially beautiful - because it isn't - or because the natives are especially friendly – because they aren't – or because she met a local boy and married, but because of the rain and the midges and the tumble-down cottage she stays in which asks nothing of her except a determination to be.

She is not the least bit interested in genealogy or in the local stories, and doesn't record anyone on her digital handset, and doesn't spend hours in the local pub, but spends her time gathering wood for the fire, harvesting bees, growing vegetables and herbs, and fishing from her creel-boat, *The Tall Building*.

A graduate in architecture, her building is now the world. Where others contrast, she compares. 'This is not an island,' she told me once, 'but a great city whose streets are endless – see the snails creep through the undergrowth! See the buzzards up there, right on top of the skyscrapers!'

'My portion of New York' she says. 'My metropolis here in the silence. Do you know that one morning I sat here and watched two crows flying in hard from the east, right into the bark of that oak tree, which crumbled into fragments from the force of their beaks?'

She is tall and beautiful, and speaks lovingly of her gentle upbringing on the east side of the river. She speaks dreamily of Aspen and Colombian coffee in the back streets of Boston and every day affirms that her existence here is no accident. She is the perfect one who has come here without guilt or expectation, neither to escape nor to possess.

We are all in love with her liberty, and the ease with which she bears the citizenship of the whole world, like a butterfly.

All is fixed and fluid, like the ocean. What you believed to be fictional was real, what you believed to be everlasting has dissolved. The imagined was false: holiday-homeland was a fable, the great escape a lie. When you opened the well-fastened suitcase, all your sins spilt out once more. The island of Free Will was really the island of Predestination, the one of Invention only that of Discovery, the one that meant nothing has come to mean all things. From the one that matters most you can travel safely furthest, because the circle is sacred and perfect.

The lost city of Atlantis flashes by, like a cartoon, through the bus window as you drive south through Eagradail making for Sharinsay where – it is said – the Fairy Flag has already fallen three times, signifying the end of the world. But you remember that in the other tradition the fabled island of Rocabarra has to appear over the ocean's edge three times before the end comes. And it has only happened once, at the time of the great drought in 1888.

Yet you somehow imagine you can return to the beginning, just to check out how they're doing on the journey back. 'How are you?' 'And have you been well?' are the great simple doors into the unknown, and to your astonishment you still find them as they were, engaged in that eternal conversation.

Have they travelled too – or even with you, despite all the deaths and changes? What marvels have happened since you've been gone? And is Haggarty still living, weaving that ever-expanding house out of crotal and kelp?

Of course he is! See him flashing gold in the sunset, and hear the squelches and the yelps in amongst the seaweed, and listen to the rocks whimper and cry.

And did you hear about the *Fir-chlisneach* – The Aurora Borealis – The Suddenly Darting Ones? And how Christina MacInnes of Coileag, Eriskay says they were kin to the fairies. 'They are angels who fell out of heaven' she said, 'the *Fir-chlisneach* and the fairies – and when the Aurora Borealis is seen darting about the sky then the *Fir-chlisneach* are fighting among themselves, and, always about that time, their blood is found on rocks on the earth. This blood is not liquid, but brown and parched and sticks to the rocks like lichen and it is called *Fuil nam Fear-chlisneach* – The Blood of the Suddenly Darting Ones.'

And the real story-gatherer asked Christina how they did not stay on the earth like the other fairies and she replied, 'When the angels were falling out of heaven, St Michael noticed that heaven was likely to be emptied of its inhabitants. So God ordered that the contest should cease and everything remain as it was, and so the angels that fell into the pit stayed there, and those that fell into the rocks remained there, and those that fell on the earth stayed there, and those that were falling in the sky remained there.'

Christina MacInnes of Coileag, Eriskay added that she was not afraid of the *Fir-chlisneach*. No more than women were afraid of the sparks which came off their bodies in the olden times when they removed their woollen clothing. Those sparks which excited the men and dazzled the children.

And why should she be afraid, because she was not afraid of herself.

And with that, the storyteller – Ivor or Haggarty or the ghosts outside the door, the one who has made, or read, the story, who can tell? – lights the lamp and switches on that other fashioned world where the natives as well as the visitors communicate to each other only via electronic waves which no-one now really believes to be either magical or supernatural.